TOMBSTONE SHOWDOWN

by

Mike Stotter

Dales Large Print Books
Long Preston, North Yorkshire,
BD23 4ND, England.

British Library Cataloguing in Publication Data.

Stotter, Mike
Tombstone showdown.

A catalogue record of this book is
available from the British Library

ISBN 978-1-84262-785-3 pbk

First published in Great Britain in 1991
by Robert Hale Limited

Published in Large Print 2010 by arrangement with
Mike Stotter

Dales Large Print is an imprint of Library Magna Books Ltd.

Printed and bound in Great Britain by
T.J. (International) Ltd., Cornwall, PL28 8RW

This one is for my parents.
You are owed far more
than just a book dedication.
Love you both.

ONE

The lead rider brought his sorrel to a halt on the lip of the wooded rise. He drew out his big .44 S&W Russian, broke open the cylinder, slid a bullet into the empty sixth chamber, then reholstered it. He hipped around in the saddle, watching as his five companions brought up the rear, shoving his hat to the back of his head and wiping his sweaty forehead with his neckerchief. The other riders reined in alongside him.

Clancy Le Duc told them, 'The stage agent's place is just over that ridge.' He indicated the direction with a nod of his head.

'What time you got now?' asked Davey Shaw.

Le Duc took out his pocket watch. 'Ten after three.' He watched the other riders shifting in their saddles, easing their butts after the rough eight-mile ride. 'Stage ain't due for another hour.'

'That's if it's on time,' said John Franklin.

'Yeah,' agreed Le Duc. 'So we might as well grab ourselves some rest.'

Stepping down out of the saddle, Le Duc said to Davey Shaw, 'Listen, what we went through last night still goes, you got it?'

Shaw nodded, adding none too enthusiastically, 'Yeah.'

'You're committed, boy,' Franklin told him sternly as he also dismounted. 'Ain't no turning back now.'

Shaw was on his feet, banging trail dust off his leather chaps. He looked up at Franklin. He was young, inexperienced, worried bad.

Clancy Le Duc sat down in the shade of some cholla. He unwrapped his sougan and took a shotgun from its folds. He broke open the Greener and loaded it with a pair of 10 gauge shells he took from his jacket pocket. He watched the rest of the men dismount and tend to their animals, polishing the dull barrels of the shotgun with the sougan as he tried to keep his mind on the job at hand.

A shadow fell across him. He looked up just as John Franklin dropped to the ground beside him. Le Duc watched him through squinting eyes. Franklin was a bear of a man. He stood over six feet tall and was almost as wide. Black hair hung down to his shoulders, and piercing green eyes surveyed the world from beneath a heavy brow. At the age of thirty-five, he claimed to have killed as many men.

'D'you think the kid'll be all right?' Franklin asked.

Le Duc looked over to Shaw. 'Reckon so.'

Franklin shook his head. 'I ain't so certain.'

'Oh, why?'

'Remember the way he backed down in that saloon in El Paso?'

Le Duc remembered it all right. It had cost the life of one of his men. And for what? Such a stupid mistake. Anyone could have made it, but it was the kid, and Franklin would never forgive him for that. But, hell, who was to know who the kid was going up against? Not everyone goes around with a US Marshal's badge pinned to his lapel. Besides, it wasn't entirely Shaw's fault. Curly shouldn't have stuck his nose in where it didn't belong. As far as Le Duc was concerned, the matter was closed. But Franklin wouldn't let it go.

'So?' said Le Duc.

Franklin cleared his throat. 'If we have to start shootin', I've a suspicion he won't back us up. I won't have him guarding my back, anyway.'

Off-handedly, Le Duc said, 'Then he'll guard mine.'

Franklin looked at him in amazement. 'I'm talking 'bout the difference 'tween living and dying here, Clance.'

'You think I don't know that?'

Franklin shook his head. 'I think you've gone loco.'

Le Duc snapped the Greener shut and began wrapping the quilted blanket back around it. He looked Franklin straight in the eye. 'Maybe I am. But I'm still the head *honcho* round here, John – not you.'

Franklin got to his feet, almost snorting with rage. He wasn't an easy man to rile, but this time, this time Le Duc was pushing him just that little bit too far. He hitched up his gunbelt and said, 'There's no need to take that tone with me!'

Franklin's raised voice was drawing the other outlaws' attention. They stopped what they were doing and formed a loose half-circle around the two men, their eyes filled with anticipation. Le Duc noticed them crowding in but remained seated. He looked up at Franklin, who had the sun silhouetting him against the cloudless blue sky.

'Your timing's all wrong,' he said quietly to the big man. 'We got a job to do, and if we get out of it in one piece and you still want to settle things, then I'll oblige you. But for now – back off.'

Franklin went to say something but bit it off when he saw Le Duc slip his forefinger around the Greener's triggers. The shotgun's twin barrels were poking out from the sougan in his direction. Franklin held his hands up, away from the tied-down Colt on his right thigh, and took a couple of steps backward. His stomach was taut with tension but his head told him to keep his peace. After all, you don't argue with a man pointing a sawn-down at you.

Le Duc gave a low sigh of relief when Franklin backed down. A donnybrook with his right-hand man was the last thing he wanted, especially today. He looked around at the other men.

'OK, show's over. Grab yourselves some coffee and rest up awhile. We'll be moving out before long, so you'd best check your guns.' He watched them move off towards the small fire where the aroma of fresh coffee wafted in the still air.

Clancy Le Duc dug into his top pocket, pulled out a fat stogie and lit up. He drew hard until the end glowed brightly, and as he blew out dense smoke that hung lazily in the Arizonan afternoon, he studied his men, the Le Duc Raiders.

The man holding the blackened coffee pot was 'Lucky' Newbury. Almost into his thirties, Lucky was short, bow-legged and plug-ugly. He'd acquired his nickname early in life after a short but ill-fated career as a horse wrangler, though no one with an ounce of sense ever brought that subject up to his bearded face. If they did, they usually ended up on their butts, nursing split lips.

Squatting down on his haunches next to Lucky was Ralph Burn. Burn was in his late thirties and the eldest of the gang. Life had taken a hard toll of him; his once-brown hair was now completely white, and time had ravaged his features. A .36 ball lodged in his skull had dimmed his lights somewhat, but although he might well have been the slowest-witted and most sullen among them, he was also the best marksman.

Bobby Hayes lay outstretched on his blanket, cleaning his Colt with his neckerchief. At over six feet five and whipcord thin, he was the tallest and best-looking of the six; his youthful features turned the head and fluttered the heart of many a woman. Dressed to match in a suit of grey with a starched white collar and shirt with a black string tie, only the twin holstered rig marred his otherwise elegant ensemble.

And lastly, there was Davey Shaw. By far the youngest of the Raiders – not yet reaching seventeen years old. It was only because his father had ridden with Le Duc for more than five years, a lifetime in their profession, that Le Duc had agreed to nursemaid the boy when Bob Shaw bought a one-way ticket to hell on their last stagecoach job. Young Davey was much like his father in many ways; blond hair, blue eyes, ruby-lipped and not a hint of stubble on his vaguely weak jaw. But in the eyes of the others he still had to prove his worthiness as a member of the Raiders.

Shaw looked up from his coffee and glanced over to the man he called boss. Le Duc motioned with a jerk of his head that Davey should join him. When the boy was near enough, Le Duc said, 'Sit down a while, Davey.'

Davey did as he was told.

'Now, son,' Le Duc began. 'We're heading for a spell of trouble between Franklin and yourself, so it's best I warn you 'bout that rattlesnake. I promised your pa that I'd do all I could to protect you and, by God, I'll live up to that promise.'

'Yes, sir.'

'For starters, you gotta keep out'n his way on this job. I've got me a feeling that iffen he gets the chance, he'll back-shoot you. Me too, come to that.'

Shaw took a sip of Arbuckle's and said, 'You? But why, Clance? He's got no quarrel with you, has he?'

Le Duc scratched at his chin and looked off into the distance. 'Maybe he's just tired of waiting around for me to catch the bullet with my name on it.'

'He's itching to take over, you mean?'

Le Duc nodded slowly. 'That's what I mean.'

Shaw threw his coffee dregs to the ground and looked up at Franklin, watching the man as he talked easily with the others but only half-listened to their answers. Davey asked, 'What can you do about him, then?'

'Ain't nothing I can do, at present.'

'You're not just going to sit around and wait till he pulls iron?'

Le Duc favoured him with a puzzled look. 'Hell, who said anything about sitting?' He got up with the sougan-wrapped Greener still in his hands. 'We're burning daylight, boys. Saddle up an' let's get this 'un done.'

They broke camp and were retightening cinches when Franklin walked over to Shaw. Although the youngster tried to ignore him, it became kind of difficult when the big man clamped a meaty hand over his right shoulder and squeezed real tight. Shaw tried to squirm his sway out of the grip but Franklin held him firm, turning the boy to face him.

Franklin leaned close. 'I'm warnin' you, boy,' he said in a low, deadly voice. 'If you go chicken on us agin like you did in El Paso, I'll kill you.'

Shaw pushed at Franklin's arm but it didn't budge. 'Let go!' he husked.

But Franklin only increased the pressure even more. His eyes were as hard as flint as he looked into Shaw's worried face. 'I ain't aimin' on pluckin' a harp 'longside Saint Peter *just* yet, boy. You may have Le Duc watching over you, but he ain't gonna be around forever. And when his time comes, I'll be waitin'. I'll be waitin' for you!'

Davey Shaw finally broke free from the grip. He blinked nervously. His heart hammered fit to bust. He tried holding the other man's stare, but failed, fixing his eyes on an old scar just above Franklin's right eyebrow instead. He'd been scared in the past for sure, but coming face to face with the likes of Franklin just frightened the hell out of him.

For one mad second Shaw toyed with the idea of hauling iron, although he knew that his hand would only brush the plain cedar butt of his .45 single-action before he adopted a prone position. He realized that the best course of action was to keep a bridle on his rising temper, and, like Le Duc, await a better moment.

Franklin saw the uncertainty in the boy's eyes and gave what could loosely be termed as a smile. He backed off a couple of places, hands dangling at his sides, watching Shaw all the while. When he knew that the youngster wouldn't draw on him, he turned away and headed for his mount.

His left hand was on the pommel and one foot in the stirrup when he was suddenly grabbed from behind and hauled off-balance. Franklin knew that there was only one sumbitch with balls enough to do that to him. He swore and turned to face Le Duc.

A straight right-hander landed on his nose, pushing him backwards into his horse. The bay snorted and moved sideways, making Franklin lose his balance again. The left cross that was meant for his temple glanced across his chin instead. He bellowed with rage, shook his head to clear it, charged at Le Duc with both arms outstretched, trying to capture him in a bear hug.

Le Duc was too canny a fighter to fall for that one, though. He neatly side-stepped to the left and brought his right boot up, crashing it into Franklin's chest.

Franklin staggered back, open-mouthed. His nose stung and his brisket felt caved-in. He gingerly touched his nose, and when he brought his hand away, the fingers were covered with blood.

'You son of a bitch!' he bellowed. 'What in hell's name you pickin' a fight with *me* for?'

Le Duc had his own breathing under control. 'I ain't got time for a flannelmouth in this set-up, John. You wanna pick on a body your own size, well, go right ahead and pick on me.'

Clancy Le Duc was almost right. His build was similar to Franklin's, but he was a shade smaller and more muscular. A drooping black moustache hung down his wide-boned face, and his black hair was cut short.

His weather-tanned face was deeply lined, so much so that it added ten years on to his thirty-five, and the S&W Russian .44 at his right thigh looked to be well-used. Right then his fingertips were scant inches away from its grips.

He looked at Franklin. 'Well?'

Franklin sensed the others watching him.

Le Duc said, 'Well, John, what's it to be? We gonna settle it here and now, or what?'

Franklin shook his head. 'Uh-huh.'

Le Duc eyed him intently. 'Then take your bay and go.'

Again Franklin shook his head. 'You're not throwin' me out?' he asked, plainly incredulous.

'That I am.'

'The hell you are!'

Le Duc smiled. 'Stop me, then.'

The other members of the Le Duc Raiders backed away from the two men, who stood only five or six feet from each other, none caring too much to catch a stray piece of lead.

Franklin stood as still as a rock, staring at Le Duc, his hand away from his pistol. 'Now wait on…'

'I'm tired of waiting, John. Of waiting for you or some other critter to put me underground. I'm not willing to ride down to that stage station and have you shoot me in the back…'

'Christ, Clance! You know I ain't no back-shooter!' Franklin shouted at him.

Le Duc sighed heavily. 'Let's cut the bull-shit and just finish it, John.'

Franklin removed his hat, wiping away the sweat from his forehead with his coat sleeve. The slight breeze that had sprung up was cool on his face but his body felt clammy. He shook his head.

'No, I'd sooner ride on,' he said quietly. 'We can settle this another time and place, Le Duc.' The aggression was back in his voice. 'I ain't finished with you, not by a long stretch.'

'That's fine with me,' Le Duc said with a grim chuckle.

Franklin put the Plainsman hat back on his head and turned to his bay. He reached out for his reins and gathered them in his left hand. Before he could mount up, though, he suddenly twisted back around, his .45 in his right hand, hammer cocked back.

The first shot boomed. Flame filled the air. The slug caught Franklin in the guts and he staggered back a couple of paces, shock plain in his face. He looked down at the blood pumping from the hole in his stomach, then snarled and began to bring the Colt up.

He never got to aim at Le Duc. The second shot hit him in the chest and sent him sprawling on to his back. He fought for breath as the blood ebbed out of him. Franklin vaguely saw Le Duc looming over him, black against the stark blue sky. He began to form an obscenity on his lips that never came out.

His eyes glazed over.

He died.

Le Duc pulled down on the S&W's barrel and exposed the cylinder. He ejected the spent .44s and fed two more cartridges into the emptied chambers, shaking his head.

'We gonna bury him?' Burn asked in the silence.

'We ain't got the time,' Le Duc answered evenly. 'Push him into the cholla and throw some rocks over him.'

Lucky Newbury eyed Franklin's saddle enviously. Le Duc saw this and nodded. In moments, Newbury had swapped his old Visalia saddle for Franklin's newer Ellenberg. Tightening the girth, Lucky said, 'Well, that's one thing in our favour.'

'What's that?' asked Hayes.

'We only got to make a five-way cut now.'

Hayes snorted. 'That all you ever think about, money and your guts?'

'Ain't nothing wrong with that. A body's got to eat, and he can't live on charity the whole of his life.'

'The only charity you live on,' Hayes said, 'is from folks with their hands scratching buzzard-belly!'

Lucky laughed as he stepped up into the Ellenberg, getting himself settled into the new leather. 'You could be right, Bobby, but it ain't a bad way to make a living!'

'All right, that's enough yammer,' Le Duc said. 'We got us some unfinished business to 'tend, so move out!'

TWO

Jim Brandon came awake with a start. For one instant he wasn't sure where he was. His tired, bleary eyes fought to adjust to the dim half-light of the hotel room. His head pounded something furious, the result of too much whiskey drunk too damn' fast.

The sun had disappeared hours ago, but light filtered into the room from the street through the flimsy curtained window. Brandon raised his throbbing head off the soft pillow and strained his ears for the sound that had woken him.

Sounds rose into the air from Allen Street. Brandon listened to the music of horses' hooves striking the hard-packed ground, the raised voices of passers-by. From downstairs, in the saloon, men enjoying themselves, and rising above the clamour, the harsh braying of a whore's false laugh. Life in Tombstone carried on regardless of the hour.

Brandon pushed up his aching body from the mattress and sat up. His eyes scanned the small dark room. He could see the ghostly shape of his gear, piled high where he had dropped it. Instinctively he knew that his Colt Lightning was still in place on top of the dresser. And above all, the door was closed.

Two muted gunblasts split the air and made him start. He jerked his head around to the window and caught the reflection of light on metal from the corner of his eye.

'What in tarnation…' he began. His voice was hoarse with cheap whiskey and cheaper cigars. Fumbling at his bedside table, he managed to trim the wick on the small lamp. Its light threw an eerie glow across the room. Brandon saw him instantly.

A Chinaman dressed in black silk robes stood in the shadows, a wicked-looking blade held in his hand. The Westerner recognized him as Jian, the first to welcome him to Tombstone.

Jim Brandon had ridden in with the Dragoon mountains behind him. The sky had been cloudless, the day hot and dry. His chestnut horse had picked its own way down the trail, and Brandon sat easy in the saddle with his feet out of the stirrups. They topped the rise and he looked down on Tombstone across a wide treeless plateau.

His journey from Gila Bend had taken him almost two weeks, and though it had been uneventful, the need to remain alert for marauding Apaches had drained him, mentally as well as physically.

It was a time for a period of recuperation.

Riding into town, what Brandon had remembered as a quietish thoroughfare was Allen Street, the now-bustling commercial centre of town. Miners, traders, and housewives all rubbed shoulders as they hurried along. It didn't take him long to find a livery that would offer his mount 'the best possible care for fifty cents a day', an offer he couldn't refuse. The ostler recommended The Cosmopolitan as a fine place to stay, and Brandon took him up on the suggestion, finding the place two blocks further up on Allen.

Brandon entered the hotel's saloon and decided that despite all its fancy decorations, it was just another frontier bar. The mahogany bartop ran the length of the back wall, mirrors hung behind it, reflecting the faces of the men drinking their fill and of the girls working their pitches.

On his way to the bar, Brandon's way was blocked by a small Chinaman, dressed in the traditional silk robes of his people, all red and gold embroidery. His hair was tied back in a pig-tail that hung beneath a head cap which matched the design of his robes.

'You stayin' here, mister?' the Chinaman asked.

'Yeah,' Brandon replied guardedly.

'I take bags and show you room, yes?'

Brandon shrugged. 'Whatever you say, but I need to cut the dust from my throat first.'

'It OK, I bring bottle to room.' He wrinkled his nose at Brandon. 'You need bath, too.'

Brandon sniffed at the air and silently agreed with the Oriental, then said, 'OK, lead the way…'

'Name's Jian. And you…?'

'Jim Brandon, from Kansas.' Adding the Kansas as if to say he didn't want to be associated with any other Brandons from any place else.

Jian ushered him through the crowd, jostling cowboys and women out of their path with his slight shoulders. He looked behind him and said to Brandon, 'You look like card player. Me right?'

Brandon laughed. 'Hell, Jian. Got me pegged from the word go, ain'tcha?'

Jian flicked his almond eyes over Brandon's taller body. 'You dress like one. Your eyes never still, an' you got gun tucked under armpit. Simple, simple.'

Brandon smiled at Jian's correct and uncanny observations. He was a gambler, all right, had been from the age of twenty. Circumstances had forced him into the profession and the more he thought of it, the more painful the memories became. He mentally shrugged off the uneasy feeling and set his sights on the present. This second visit to Tombstone was professionally motivated. He'd heard tales of a private detective-cum-gambler named Luke Heller. And, if what folks said about him were true, then any encounter they were likely to have across a baize-topped table would be a game to remember.

He'd also been warned about the Earp brothers and their cronies, but so long as he kept his nose clean and the game fair, he guessed that there'd be no trouble.

Now, with Jian's suggestion of a hot bath and a comfortable bed, the thoughts he had harboured about the game were diminishing. He followed the little man with the swaying pig-tail up the stairs. Jian took him into a single room off by the balcony. It was a spartan affair; a dresser, wardrobe and wash-stand. A large tin bath was already positioned at the foot of the wide bed.

Jian put Brandon's gear on to the floor, and bowing, he said, 'Is there anything else?'

Brandon thought for a moment before saying, 'I'll have that bottle of whiskey you promised, then you can fill the bath.'

The Chinaman suddenly leered. 'You want girl?'

'Uh?'

'Want nice girlie? She very clean, honest.'

Although the thought had crossed Brandon's mind when he had entered the hotel, and saw the girls at work, he hadn't formulated any firm plans in that direction.

'No, thanks.'

'Want boy?' Jian persisted.

'Hell, no!' Brandon fought to keep his temper from rising. He breathed out heavily and said, 'D'you know where I can find a high-staked card game 'round here?'

Jian nodded. He leaned closer to Brandon, and in a voice just above a whisper, he said, 'Go to Freemont Street. Second house on left past the Bauer's place is Strong's.

They've got a place in back, very high stakes, and their games go on till early hours. You tell them I sent you.'

Brandon smiled. 'I ain't worried 'bout the time. So long as it's a good and fair game, I don't really care. I'm obliged to you, Jian.'

But the Chinaman was wrong. Jim Brandon's plans for a good game hadn't panned out right. The stakes weren't that high and the opposition was amateurish. There was no challenge and after a while he'd grown vaguely embarrassed in taking every pot. Now he began to ache from the long journey and he excused himself from the game, despite the cries from the other players wanting to be given the chance to win some of their money back.

It was just turned midnight when Brandon finally lowered himself into bed and wrapped the sheets around him. He had thought no more about Jian – not until now.

The Chinaman's face remained impassive. His eyes held Brandon's in a steady gaze.

'What the hell d'you think you're…' Brandon's voice had an edge to it. But he stopped speaking when Jian ignored him and stepped further into the room. Brandon could see the danger dancing behind his eyes. His own eyes slipped to the evil-looking pig-sticker which Jian was brandishing menacingly. 'You got any intentions of using that?'

Jian said, 'Who knows?'

Brandon shook his head. He watched Jian advance towards him, raising the knife shoulder-high. He tensed as the adrenalin began pumping through his body. In a single movement he was off the bed and grabbing for the empty whiskey bottle. He swung it down on the bedside table, showering the floor with glass. At least now he had a weapon of his own, the jagged bottle-neck.

Jian's eyes narrowed even further as he stopped in his tracks. His confidence drained slightly. Jian had been informed about the gambler's winnings and he needed that money. If he had to kill him to get it, then he would. All he cared for was the money. That's why he threw good sense out of the window and lunged at Brandon.

The knife hissed through the air, missing the top of Brandon's head by a scant inch. He, in turn, ducked and swung the bottle-neck at Jian's stomach in a sweeping arc, but the Oriental danced easily out of the way. They faced each other again. Brandon feinted to his left and brought his weapon up in a stabbing move at Jian's legs. The Chinaman hopped back and let Brandon's momentum carry him by, then brought the knife down on Brandon's forearm.

Brandon saw the move at the last moment and dodged out of the way, jumping over the bathtub to put it between himself and the Chinaman. Now he could reach for the Colt. He threw the bottle-neck over-handed at Jian. The Chinaman ducked as the remains of the bottle sailed over his head and smashed harmlessly against the wall behind him. At the same time, Brandon raced to the dresser and grabbed for his Colt.

'Hold it right there, you sonofabitch!'

Brandon shouted, aiming the Colt at the Chinaman's face. 'Drop the blade.'

Jian's face drained of all colour. It wasn't so much fear that coursed through his mind and body as he stared down the barrel of the pistol. It was sheer terror. He released the knife.

'What's the idea?' Brandon asked, not really expecting an answer.

Jian's eyes were ablaze with anger. He stepped forward, a twisted sneer on his face.

Brandon eared back the hammer, his stomach tense. Angry and scared at the same time. 'Hold it there, chink.'

Jian stopped just inches away from the gun barrel, his eyes boring into Brandon's. Then he moved. Quicker than Brandon would have thought possible.

Jian took a step to the left, at the same time bending his body forward, away from the gun, and brought his right hand down on Brandon's gun wrist.

The vicious karate chop made Brandon lower the gun but he fought to hold on to it.

Jian pivoted and brought his left hand to grab Brandon's right wrist, his right bending back Brendon's right thumb. Then he pulled hard on the gun hand, twisting it at the same time.

Brandon let out a cry as the Colt Lightning was wrenched from his grip. The whole of his right hand seemed on fire. Now the Chinaman had gotten him mad. Real mad.

The force of his attack had made Jian turn sideways to Brandon. He was confident enough to believe that the Westerner would not wish to continue the fight. But he was wrong. He grunted as Brandon's punch connected with his lower ribs, and began to turn, gun in hand. Brandon had already expected that move; his good hand wrapped around Jian's right sleeve and he pulled hard.

Now Jian was off balance, falling forwards. Brandon ducked under his body and lifted him up on his shoulder, twisting his body at the same time.

Brandon had taken enough from the little man, and continued to lift Jian's body to throw him out of the window. The Chinaman made no noise as he crashed through the glass and thudded down onto the hard ground below.

Jim Brandon looked down at the broken body. The cold night air blasted through the window, drying his sweating body. His breathing was hard and ragged but he knew that he had to get away. He could feel the panic rising in him.

Townsfolk were stopping to look at the dead Chinaman. Brandon turned as he heard the soft creak of a loose floorboard behind him. He felt the cold of gun metal pressing against his kidneys. He swallowed hard and struggled for breath. Cautiously he looked down at the twin-barrelled Remington threatening him.

'Hold it, mister. Make a wrong move an' I'll be plastering you all over town.' The soft Irish lilt did nothing to alleviate Brandon's rising fear. 'Turn around, nice and slowly like. No shenanigans, or I'll pull both triggers, that I will.'

Brandon turned slowly and faced the man with the shotgun. The Irishman was a big fellow, all red beard and muscles. The Remington looked like a child's toy in his big, calloused hands.

'Now, Irish. Hold up one minute,' Brandon began. 'It ain't like it seems.'

'Bastard!' the Irishman said tersely. Then brought the shotgun barrels down on the side of Brandon's neck.

Silently, Brandon fell to the floor in an untidy heap.

The room was dark and uncomfortably cold when Brandon regained consciousness. His vision was blurred when he cracked his eyes open and it took him a few seconds for them to focus. He winced as he put his weight on his right shoulder and tried to push himself upright. The shoulder gave way and he fell back down with a soft moan.

Somewhere off in the distance he heard muffled gunshots and plenty of shouting. Moving slowly, he finally got himself upright. Each movement bringing him pain. He touched his sore, stiff neck. When his eyes adjusted to the gloom he didn't like what he saw.

The inside of a prison cell.

He slowly shook his head to clear it. Standing up he called out, 'Hey! Anyone out there?' His voice was hoarse within the confines of the windowless cell. The only light filtered in from beneath the wooden door set in the cell-block wall. He walked up to the cell door, and it registered in his mind that he was dressed in just his combinations. He looked around and saw his clothes piled up on the metal bunk. Carefully, so as not to aggravate his injuries, he dressed himself. From the other side of the wood door he could hear movement.

'Is anyone there?' he called out again.

This time his shouting was answered. The cell-block door opened and someone stood in the doorway. Brandon could not make out any features in the darkness, just the outline of a small, hatless man.

Brandon asked, 'What the hell's going on?'

'You're under arrest, mister.'

'I guessed that,' he said sarcastically. 'What for?'

The man in the shadows laughed. 'What for? Don't tell me your brain's been addled.' He turned and called over his shoulder, 'Ellis, c'mere. This one don't know why he's here – playing the innocent.'

The man called Ellis walked up to his fellow jailer. 'What's he saying, Dutch?'

'Why not ask me?' invited Brandon.

Ellis laughed. 'Don't get uppity, boy. You're here because you've been up to no good.' His harsh nasal twang betrayed his Eastern origins. Brandon figured that he was probably from New York. Just another immigrant who'd drifted West to find his fortune.

Brandon's jaw muscles worked hard, slowly relaxing as he told himself to calm down. Again he asked, 'What for?'

Dutch walked further into the room and into the overspill of light. The first thing that caught Brandon's eye was the deputy badge pinned to his vest pocket. The second was the sawn-off Remington he was holding on his right thigh. Dutch stood three paces from Brandon's cell door.

Brandon waited. His hands were balled tightly into fists. He stared at Dutch, studying the deputy's face. It was a squat face with a full, untrimmed beard hiding his lower jaw. Heavy-hooded eyes returned Brandon's stare, waiting for him to look away, but Brandon didn't.

'Listen, feller,' Dutch said, breaking the silence, 'in case you don't recall, I'll remind you of what you did over at The Cosmopolitan tonight. A Chinaman was thrown out of the window, snapping his spine. You killed him.'

'Me? Now listen, you've got this all wrong...'

'Oh?'

'Damn' right! It was the Chinaman...'

'The dead Chinaman?'

Brandon heard the scepticism in the

deputy's voice. He shook his head in dismay. 'I only acted in self-defence against the Chinaman.'

Ellis now stood next to Dutch. They matched each other in height, though Ellis was clean shaven, his eyes more alert looking. Brandon thought he looked like an eagle.

Ellis said, 'You'll face a murder charge, Brandon. The sheriff's pretty hot about folks messing up his town.'

'That goes for us, too,' Dutch said.

Brandon backed away from the cell door, rubbing at the bridge of his nose with thumb and forefinger. 'Give me some time to think,' he said.

Ellis looked at him. 'Oh, you'll have plenty of time for that, Brandon. Sheriff Behan's due back shortly, and I'm sure he'll want to talk with you.'

'You charging me with murder, right?' Brandon asked.

Dutch said, 'That's about the size of it.'

Brandon grunted, then said, 'In that case,

get me a lawyer.'

'Not until the sheriff's seen you.'

'Hey, I've got rights, you know.'

Dutch shook his head. 'You've got as much rights as we see fit to give you.'

Brandon said, 'If you fellers're so all-fired sure I'm a killer, the least you can do is give me access to a lawyer.'

Dutch wiped his hand through his beard and smiled. 'Now listen here, mister,' he said, moving a little closer to the cell bars. 'No one gives us orders. *You're* the one behind these here bars, not us. Take one step out of line and you won't know what's hit you.'

Brandon reached out and held the bars tightly. His gaze moved from Ellis to Dutch, taking his time. His eyes held on Dutch as he said softly, 'You don't scare me. Anyone with an ounce of sense could see that I didn't kill the Chinaman on purpose. It's a straight case of self-defence. What reason would I have? Money? No, I won enough to pay both your wages for the next year...'

Ellis said, 'There weren't no money in the room.'

Brandon hesitated, thinking. 'Christ, I don't believe this!' He turned away from the deputies and stepped further back into his cell. Then he stopped. He was in deep trouble. He had to explain everything calmly, logically, try to win these characters over. Quickly he told them about his first meeting with Jian, of that evening's card game, and Jian's attempt to rob him, and the ensuing fight.

When he'd finished telling them Ellis shook his head and smiled. 'You'll have to do better than that, Brandon. Straight out of some dime novel.'

Brandon sighed heavily and looked at Ellis, deciding there and then that he didn't particularly care for the small Easterner. In fact, nothing would have given him greater pleasure than reaching through the bars and grabbing him by the throat.

'Listen, at least do me one favour,' he said. 'Go over to The Cosmopolitan and have a word with the manager. I bet that he's had this kind of trouble before.'

'Already been taken care of,' Dutch said, walking away.

Brandon shot him a puzzled look.

'The sheriff's over at the hotel, sorting things out,' Ellis explained.

Brandon watched the door swing shut and turned back into his cell. He looked at the metal-framed crib and the single dirt-encrusted blanket and decided that it was cleaner to sit on the floor. The stone was cool on his back as he stretched out his long legs in front of him and closed his eyes.

Not to sleep but to gather his thoughts.

THREE

The four span of mules pulled hard in their traces as Ol' Man White cracked his bull-whip above their heads, urging more speed out of them as they careered up the steep grade leading out of the barranca. Foam flecked their dusty hides as they struggled to meet the new demands. White cursed them loudly, disregarding the passengers in the coach and their complaints about his colourful language.

'Gawdam you stupid sons of ... pull this here crate!' he bellowed. White used the whip once more as they reached the ridge of the barranca, and with an almighty effort the mules pulled the ancient mud wagon over the lip and out on to more even ground.

Ol' Man White turned to Larry Whipple, his shotgun rider, and shouted in his ear,

'Told you these here mules were worth their weight in gold!'

Whipple held on to the side rail as the stage ran over a stretch of rough ground. 'Yeah – and you'll be the death of 'em yet!'

'The hell I will!' White shouted back. 'These mules are the finest the company's bought in years.'

'Perhaps it's something to do with you choosing 'em?' Whipple teased.

White gave his shotgun rider a withering look and spat a wad of phlegm over the side of the box. At forty-three, he was the oldest driver that Wells, Fargo employed on this particular run, but the way the journey shook up his innards, he felt more like sixty-three. The sun had done its best to burn his skin to a cinder and the constant exposure to the changing elements had turned his face into a Lewis and Clarke pencil map. A thick white beard covered the lower half of his face and his piercing blue eyes set under shaggy brows were all Whipple had had of any interest to look at since leaving Benson.

Not that Whipple was any oil painting himself. Having just crept into his mid-twenties, life had dealt with him harshly. Cross-eyed and hare-lipped, he had managed to come to terms with both, but he still hated being called a hunchback. His dry sense of humour usually dispelled any adversity aimed at him – that and his well-packed biceps.

The stagecoach slowed down a pace and White stowed the long bullwhip away, allowing the mules to keep their fast pace without further encouragement. The animals knew this stretch of country well, and in the evening light they followed the rutted, dirt road unerringly.

White turned his head and shouted in Whipple's ear, 'I hope that Mrs Cooke's made up her usual batch of sourdoughs. I don't think there's a body can make 'em better than she.'

The thought of the fresh sourdoughs made Whipple's mouth water. He could almost taste them. 'I could do with something right now.'

White smiled behind his beard. 'Only four miles to go and we'll be right there,' he said. 'You'd best let them folks know they'll be able to stretch their legs in thirty minutes or so.'

Whipple leaned over the side to sing out the message, which was greeted by a shout of acknowledgement.

'I'll be glad to stretch my legs, too!' Whipple called to his driver.

White shook his head. 'Hell, boy. Anyone would think you're the old man around here.' Not allowing for the fact that it was Whipple's first outing as a shotgun rider.

'The way you drive this crate makes me feel old!'

'You ever fancy walking the rest of the way?' White replied.

'Not particularly.'

''Ary you feel the need to keep on ribbin' me, son, you'll find out what it's like to be a mule!'

Whipple sucked at his teeth and let the warning wash over him. He knew that it was useless to argue with the old man when he was in such a foul mood. Travelling three or four hundred miles together had taught him that. So he let it go. Instead he looked off across the expanse of mesquite and the thickets of chapparal which seemed, in places, impenetrable.

He was also on the look-out for Apaches. The cut-throats were apt to attack stage-coaches more often in these hard times and if it wasn't them, it was some nameless, faceless gang. Oft-times, riding shotgun wasn't that all-so-easy job that Wells, Fargo had made it out to be when he'd first signed on.

Twenty minutes later the mud wagon rounded the bend and the way-station came into view. It was a welcoming sight for White and Whipple.

'Station coming up, folks!' bellowed White. He thought he heard someone call out 'at last' but ignored the caustic remark.

As they neared Cooke's Station White felt a mite uneasy and shifted in his seat. Whipple gave a look of concern and asked what was wrong. White had his head cocked to one side, staring at the adobe building gradually rocking closer.

White said, 'Can't figure it.'

Whipple rubbed at his chin. 'I can't rightly see what you mean. Nothing's happening.'

'Gawdammit, that's just it!'

'What?'

'*Nothing's* happening!'

Whipple turned from studying White's profile and shaded his eyes with his left hand, his right hand maintaining its grip on his shotgun. Looking over the station, he failed to see any sign of life. None of the Cookes to be seen, no mules in the corral, not a lamp lit; in fact nothing was moving at all.

'Pee-culiar,' Whipple muttered, dragging back both hammers of the shotgun and resting it across his thighs.

White heard the dry clicking of the hammers being cocked and shifted uneasily. 'I hope there ain't gonna be any call for you to let loose with that scattergun,' he said to Whipple. 'Just remember there's women about, and that the dudes with 'em ain't worth spit.'

'Meaning?'

'Iffen you're figuring on using that piece, you better not rely on any back-up from 'em.'

Ol' Man White turned the stage into the yard and pulled on the brake lever, but he remained seated, eyes scouring the dusty yard. He felt the wagon sway beneath him as the passengers prepared to disembark. Turning around he called out, 'Wait on, folks.'

'This is our stop, isn't it driver?' A female voice enquired.

'Yes ma'am, but I'd rather you stay put until...'

'Until what?' The voice came from the half-opened doorway leading into the adobe.

'Who's that?' asked White, squinting through the gathering darkness. 'That you, Cooke?'

A man stepped away from the door and into the gloom of the remuda. The deepening shadows concealed his face. 'Get down out of the box, old man,' he commanded.

White said, 'Who the hell d'you...'

A second voice off to his right sang out. 'Do as you're told, an' all'll be well.'

White swung his head around in the direction of the new voice and saw a tall man dressed in an ankle-length duster, whose nose and mouth were covered by a neckerchief. The man stepped out from between the adobe and the barn. There was light enough to see the Colt pointed at him.

White swallowed noisily. 'Son of a...'

The man under the remuda spoke again, 'Git down, old-timer. And you–' he nodded at Whipple, 'lose that shotgun.'

The shotgun rider looked at White for help and the older man slowly nodded. Whipple's shoulders sagged, and he began to carefully raise the shotgun from his lap. In what appeared to him as a quick piece of thinking, Larry Whipple jerked the Greener around, barrels pointing at the man with the drawn pistol and pulled the triggers.

The duster-clad outlaw must have been

reading his mind, because as the barrels came to bear down on him, he dropped to one knee and let off a shot. The bullet caught Whipple in the face and blew the back of his head apart like a ripe melon.

'Sweet Jesus!' White whispered.

Female screams came from inside the coach, ripping the air apart louder than the shotgun blast. White quickly regained his composure. 'OK ladies, let's keep things nice 'n' easy and do like they say.'

The man under the remuda threw back his head and laughed. 'That's right, old-timer. Pacify them she-males. I want everyone out of the stage and up against them corral bars. *Now!*'

White lowered himself gingerly to the ground, taking the time to kick the frost out of his joints before he got the side door open. He held out his hand for the first woman and told her gently to stand aside. He did likewise for the other two women, and watched as they stood huddled together at the corral.

The man stepped off the boards and into the yard. 'Obliged, ladies,' he said, bowing to them. 'My colleagues will be around and I'd like you to contribute to their welfare.' He turned to White, his tone hardening. 'Get the men out next, and iffen anyone gets the idea of playing the hero, my partners won't hesitate to shoot the women.'

White sneaked a look out of the corner of his eye. Now three more outlaws were appearing out of the dusk. Each carried a weapon that was pointed at the trio of women, and each man wore a neckerchief over his lower face, his hat pulled low shadowing his eyes. White did his best to look at each one of them without appearing to do so at all, trying to find something to keep in mind to identify them later. But his attention was brought back to their spokesman.

'You,' Le Duc said to White. 'Unbuckle your belt and get rid of that iron.'

White found that his hands were shaking as he fumbled with the belt buckle, eventually divesting himself of his pistol. He heard

Le Duc say, 'You men! Get out of the coach with your hands on your heads. Any funny business and them ladies won't be recognized by their own mothers!'

'OK mister,' the first man said as he stepped down out of the coach. 'Don't do anything hasty. We're doing like you tell us.'

Le Duc sauntered up to White and said, 'Don't panic old-timer, you're shaking like an autumn leaf.' He stopped about four feet away from the stagecoach driver and White believed he could see the man smiling at him. 'We ain't here to do any harm to no one.'

White said, 'No?'

'That's right.'

'What about Whipple there, with his brains filling up the boot?'

Le Duc shook his head slowly. 'He was warned. I done told him to get rid of the shotgun, but no, he wouldn't listen. Wanted to play the big man.'

White said, 'Whipple weren't no hero. Just happened to be a mite deaf, was all.'

Le Duc sucked in a deep breath and held

it for a second. 'That's pure bad luck mister. Just do like I say and there won't be any more killing.'

White looked him square in the eyes. 'What have you done with the Cookes?'

'Nothing. They're in the 'dobe. They haven't been harmed.'

'You better not've harmed 'em,' White growled, pulling himself up to his full height.

Le Duc's eyes hardened. 'Don't push me, mister. I ain't got a lot of time left.'

'Literally?' White enquired.

Le Duc frowned, and eyed him suspiciously, not quite knowing whether White was threatening him or otherwise.

They locked stares for a minute, then Le Duc spoke. 'Go lead them women over to the barn. Get them inside one stall and stay there with 'em.'

White said, 'What 'bout the Cookes?'

Le Duc turned his back on White. As he walked back to the stage station he said over his shoulder, 'They'll be joining you in a minute.'

White moved slowly over to the women, his mind in turmoil, wondering what action, if any, he should take. The other bandits had taken the loot from the women and off the two men and stood to one side, guarding the passengers who had huddled together for safety.

He glanced back over his shoulder when he heard voices behind him, and turned to see the Cookes coming out of their home with Le Duc keeping a pace or two behind them, his pistol held loosely against his thigh. In his other hand he carried a lighted lantern. He indicated that they should join the others up against the corral bars. Mrs Cooke had been crying. Her eyes were red-rimmed and puffy. But none of the family had been harmed, and White breathed a sigh of relief at that.

Clancy Le Duc stood in front of his captives, holstered his pistol, and pushed his hands into his waistband, like he was saying, 'Look, no guns. I ain't here to harm you.' He cocked his head to one side and said, 'All right; this is what's gonna happen.' He looked along the line of expectant faces. One of the women was in tears, dabbing at her eyes with a lace handkerchief. Le Duc ignored her. 'Won't one of you be hurt, I can promise you that. But that's as long as you do like I tell you. All we need is a little co-operation from *him.*' He nodded at White. 'And that's all. For everyone's safety, you're gonna be locked in that barn, yonder.'

'Till when?' asked Paul Cooke, the station agent.

Le Duc shrugged his shoulders. 'Till someone passes by and hears you.'

'Jesus, Mary and Joseph!' White exclaimed. 'Next stage ain't due here till next Thursday; three days hence.'

'You can't be so barbaric as to leave us to the buzzards, young man,' sobbed the woman who had been crying.

Le Duc looked at her. 'Ma'am, you so ugly, I'd say the buzzards'd leave you alone in case *you* eat *them!*'

His men joined him in laughter, but trailed off as Paul Cooke stepped forward, facing up to Le Duc. 'You can't do this,' he said. 'My wife's expecting. She just can't simply be dumped into a barn on the off-chance that someone'll hear us.'

Bobby Hayes stepped in front of Cooke, towering over the shorter man, and thrust the butt of his Winchester into Cooke's stomach. The agent doubled over, gasping for breath. Hayes struck him over the head with the rifle barrel and stepped back as Cooke slumped unconscious to the ground.

His wife, Janet Cooke, broke away from the small group but only got three paces before White stepped in front of her, took her by the arms and held her fast. He shook his head slowly, saying, 'Don't give 'em cause to do anything foolish, Janet. They only want me, God knows why. So just you calm down in case something happens to that little 'un inside o' you. Don't forget little Jimmy over there, either. He needs his maw and paw right now, 'cause iffen that was me, I'd be scared as hell 'bout what's going on.'

Janet managed a half-smile and back-handed away the fresh tears forming at her eyes. She said softly, 'OK Jethro, I hear you.' Then turned and walked back to her son and cradled him to her.

'That's right, old-timer,' Le Duc said. 'Look after the woman.'

White spun around to face him, eyes burning hatred. 'Her old man had a point, mister. What you gonna do about her?'

All eyes were on Le Duc. He closed his, thinking for a moment. White wished he had the courage to punch him straight in the mouth. It would feel good, but he knew the feeling wouldn't last long. A second later he would be weighed down with lead, so he bit on his lower lip, biding his time.

Le Duc opened his eyes and said, 'She'll go back into the 'dobe, but we'll lock the door and bar the windows. The boy can take care of her.' He turned to Hayes and Burn. 'See to them. You others, herd that bunch into the barn. Meanwhile, mister,' he stepped closer to White, their hat brims almost touching, 'you come with me.'

FOUR

Sheriff John Behan slumped back in his Douglas chair, one leg draped over the side, his fingers toying with his black string tie. His hard brown eyes avoided those of Brandon, who stood with his hands cuffed behind his back on the other side of the office. Dutch Larkin stood with his back resting against the rifle-rack, arms folded in front of him, and Ellis Goldbaum gazed out of the window, watching the street.

'I've been thinking about you,' Behan said, breaking the silence. He was in his mid-twenties or early thirties: it was hard to tell, what with his youthful looks. His brown hair was slicked down and parted to one side; a small goatee beard covered his pointed chin and he had begun to grow a moustache to keep it company. He was handsome in his own way, but seemed uncomfortable in Brandon's urbane presence. He stopped playing with his tie, smoothed it down and adjusted his jacket. 'As much as I'd like to, I can't just let you go.'

Brandon nodded. 'You think I'll damage your reputation, is that it?'

Behan smiled, spreading his hands. 'Something like that.'

Brandon said, 'I can't see where there's a problem. You spoke to the manager, didn't you?'

'Uh-uh.'

'Then what's the problem?'

'Not so much as an immediate problem, but I've got me a dead Chinese on my hands,' Behan sighed.

Brandon turned to face Larkin, then Goldbaum; drawing blank looks from both of them. There was an uneasy feeling settling in his stomach and he sensed there was something else going on. An undercurrent of deceit. More than just a problem with a dead Chinaman and an uncooperative manager.

Brandon glanced back at the sheriff and asked, 'What's his problem?'

Behan swung his leg back to the floor and leaned across the desk, his fingers interlocking. 'He says that this Jian feller might have been tipped off by some friends at that place he recommended to you, but he ain't swearing to it. I'm inclined to believe him.' He paused to take the time to select a thin cheroot off his desk top and lighted it.

For a moment Brandon waited and stared at the sheriff. 'D'you mind getting to the point?' he said irritably.

Behan smiled lazily at the gambler. 'He says that there weren't no witnesses when you threw the Chinaman out of the window…' Leaving the sentence hanging on its implications.

Jim Brandon closed his eyes, trying to remember. Everything had happened so quickly. The situation wasn't looking so good to him.

He swallowed loudly. 'Now everything depends on your believing in whether or not

I acted in self-defence, eh?'

Behan spread out his hands. 'What can I say?'

Brandon stood for a moment, forcing himself to breathe slowly, knowing that any moment his temper might get the better of him. 'Is that all you can say: "What can I say?" How about, "I'm letting you go through lack of evidence?" That's got a nice ring to it.'

Behan shifted in his chair. His lips forced into a tight line as he coldly eyed Brandon. He held his breath for a beat, then said, 'Seems like we've got ourselves a peculiar situation here. Most of your money's been recovered...'

'What d'you mean, *most?*'

'Expenses and the like. You get my drift?'

Brandon felt his face flush red. Not trusting himself, he clenched his fists tightly and kept his silence.

Behan said, 'I suggest the best thing for you to do, Mister Brandon, is to take the next stage out of Tombstone.'

Larkin shot his employer a puzzled frown. 'But boss,' he stammered.

The starpacker held up a hand to silence him. 'It's OK, Dutch,' he said. 'I don't think we'll have any more trouble from Mister Brandon, will we?'

'No,' answered Brandon through clenched teeth. He turned his back to Larkin, offering him his cuffed hands. 'Now unlock these things.'

The deputy pushed himself away from the rifle-rack, unfolded his arms and brought out his key. 'If it were up to me,' he said softly, 'you'd stay behind bars.'

Brandon rubbed at his reddened wrists, and turned to face Larkin. 'You know something, Dutch?' He matched Larkin's soft tone. 'You're just a dime-a-time deputy. Your word ain't worth horse shit.'

Larkin took a step towards him. 'Shut up.'

'I'll go as far in saying that I bet you'd find my missing cash under your mattress.'

'Shut up, I said.'

'That's enough!' Behan said, standing up.

Dutch Larkin was two paces away from Brandon when he cocked his fist and took a swing at Brandon's head. The gambler saw it coming a mile off and stepped out of the way. He ducked under Larkin's swinging left and shot out a stabbing right into the deputy's stomach.

He watched as Larkin doubled over, ready to give him some more, when the feel of cold iron pressing against the side of his throat brought him up sharp. Behan had come up on his blind side and was smiling at him.

'OK, boy,' Behan said. 'This has gone far enough. You got a beef with Dutch, then that's between the two of you. Now you start to accuse me of something illegal, and I don't like it. I get by on what I'm paid. I got no cause to be tempted to play on the wrong side of this badge. I make enough money on the percentage I get from collecting the taxes…'

'You don't have to explain anything to me,' Brandon said.

'I do, because you think I'm crooked. I'm not, and I don't like to be so accused. I got my own corral that pays enough to keep me in fancy suits. I'm the sheriff for this whole country, and that's an almighty powerful position to hold. I'm not looking for petty cash – politics is where the real power lies, and this,' he hooked a thumb at his badge, 'this is my stepping-stone right to the top.'

Brandon nodded towards Ellis and Dutch. 'Why vouch for them?'

'Because they get the rough end of the stick. I prefer to leave all the gunplay to them. Do you know how many deputies Tombstone has had since I've been sheriff? No, you couldn't even guess it. Fifty-two. Fifty-two men, sweating out their days and nights for not much more than three dollars a week. I can tell you that it's no fun being shot at, beaten up or riding for five days and nights in a posse and coming back with nothing but blisters on your ass!'

The pistol was quickly removed from Brandon's throat, and he breathed a deep sigh of relief. Behan now stood in front of him, slapped Brandon's face with his left hand and laid the pistol barrel across the side of Brandon's head.

The luckless gambler sprawled out on the floor.

Turning to Larkin, Behan said, 'Lock him up again, and make sure he gets on that stage.' Then he left the office without a further word.

Jim Brandon's arms were held fast. Ellis Goldbaum was holding one arm, Dutch Larkin the other, and between them they marched him out of the jail. The swollen lump over Brandon's right brow had half-closed his eye but he still recognized the stocky figure of Sheriff John Behan angling across the street towards him.

Behan halted a couple of paces away, the light from the outside lanterns throwing a yellow cast over his humourless features. He waited with hands in his pockets until Ellis and Dutch brought their man nearer, then said to Brandon, 'I'm putting you on that wagon.'

Brandon looked into the fish-like eyes. 'I 'spose there ain't no use in arguing with you, sheriff?'

'I reckon you're right. I'll give it to you straight, Brandon. I ain't got the time or inclination to keep looking over my shoulder for you to pop out of some dark alleyway and bushwhack me. I got more than enough to worry about with the Earps an' all. So, you ride out of Tombstone, and I don't expect to see you back here. Leastways, not whilst I'm sheriff.'

'Careful, sheriff.' Brandon's tone carried a hard edge. 'It's never wise to push a man into a corner.'

Behan's eyes hardened. 'Meaning?'

'Well, you go and do that, then a body ain't got no choice but to come back out fighting.'

'Are you threatening me?'

'Hell, no.' Brandon laughed, sensing the tension from the two deputies. 'Just a friendly piece of advice, is all.'

'You can shove your advice up your ass!' Behan jerked his chin at Dutch, and said, 'Get him over to the Cosmopolitan and on to that stage. I want him out of here afore I do something irresponsible.'

The deputies were only too pleased to oblige, half-carrying and half-dragging Brandon between them the rest of the way down Allen Street. Behan followed at a more sedate pace, his eyes darting from one boardwalk to another, taking deep breaths to control his rising anger.

He had already seen Jethro White and warned him to expect an extra body. The whip had complained that the stage was already full, but Behan persuaded a passenger to take the morning stage. Though he had grumbled bitterly, the ten-dollar bill Behan gave him eased the inconvenience, and the passenger gathered his gear, then sauntered off.

As they neared the stage, the deputies pushed Brandon away from them, slamming him against the side of the mud wagon. The gambler spun on his heels, hands clenched into fists as he faced up to Larkin. The deputy smiled, stained teeth grinning at him through his beard. His eyes dared Brandon to do something about it. His hand was draped over the butt of his tied-down Colt.

Behan quickly stepped between them, not wanting any unnecessary gunplay. He locked stares with Brandon.

'The taxpayers are forking out for your one-way trip, Brandon. I've given orders to the driver that you're not to get off anyplace but Contention. From there, you're entitled to go anywhere you please.'

Brandon said, 'Anywhere apart from Tombstone, that is.'

The starpacker smiled. 'That's right. And by the way; I've kept your horse to pay for your expenses – your keep, the Chinaman's burial and such. Your outfit's been stowed on top.'

'And my guns?'

'They're up there, too. 'Case you didn't

know it, there's a town ordinance about carrying hardware. I wouldn't want to arrest you for violating it.'

Brandon fixed him with a hard stare, knowing that he'd come across a mean individual. To buck him any further might prove fatal, but never one to forget a mistreatment, Brandon promised himself retribution some other time, some other place. He removed his hat and gently massaged the throbbing lump above his brow. His eyes were still fixed on Behan.

The sheriff dropped his hand onto his pistol and eased it out, thumbing back the hammer. 'Get on board,' Behan ordered. His hand was steady as he aimed at the gambler's stomach.

A tense silence enveloped the men. Brandon licked at his dry, cracked lips, then shrugged. He knew there was no point in pushing it any further.

A lazy smile spread across Behan's face as he watched Brandon pull himself into the mud wagon. The sheriff pulled down the canvas flap and fastened it securely. He walked around to the whip and looked up at him.

'OK, Jethro. Get this pile of wood outta here.'

White looked down at the lawman and grunted. He released the handbrake and slapped the leathers across the mules' backs. Behan stepped back out of the way of the turning wheels and quickly glanced at the shotgun rider – a man that he had never seen before. Then the wagon was bouncing its way up Allen. Behan shrugged, and let out a huge sigh of relief.

Dutch and Ellis relaxed their bodies and watched the stage leave town. Turning around they saw that Behan had left them in the middle of the street and was making his way back to this office.

Dutch said, 'This has kinda messed things up.'

'Ain't that the truth.'

They began walking down the street, both men thinking of what to say. When he spoke,

Dutch's voice was low and scratchy. 'Things have gotten out of hand. I don't see how we gonna get word out to him an' give fair warning.'

Ellis shook his head. 'We got us a deal, we can't back out of it now.'

'No one said we was.' Dutch was thinking hard. 'I suppose we'd better wait for John to turn in and ride out with the bad news.'

'Hold on, Dutch. One more body ain't gonna make much difference now, is it?'

Larkin turned to study his fellow lawman, seeing the tiredness in his eyes and deciding that what Ellis was saying was true.

Ellis sighed. 'We'd be better off letting this thing run its course. The outcome'll be the same, won't it?'

Dutch shrugged. 'I reckon.'

Where was his luck when he needed it?

Jim Brandon sat on the hard, uncomfortable wooden seat, his back to the whip. Being last into the stage, he'd been given the most uncomfortable place on board. He was also sandwiched between a youngster of sixteen or so and a tall dude who was all elbows and legs.

Opposite him was a cowboy around Brandon's own age, with a pushed-in face. He'd been snoring ever since they'd left Tombstone. But it was the two women who interested him the most.

They were both good looking, but the younger one was the most beautiful woman he had ever seen. Her fine features were softly tanned from the sun, and her lush black hair suggested Spanish-Mexican heritage. Her eyes were bovine-like and of a gentle shade of hazel, topped with thick, long lashes. Brandon guessed her age to be no more than twenty. She wore a skirt to her ankles, an embroidered white blouse and a black scarf that covered her delicate shoulders.

Her companion was more than eight to ten years older. She too was very good looking. She also wore simple travel clothes, and her black hair was brushed back behind her temples. Her head was held high, her firm chin regally held.

Brandon wondered if any of the men were with them and decided that they weren't, mainly because they were all *gringos* without a Mexican amongst them. Even so, he didn't dismiss the idea that the snoring cowboy may have been their protector.

There was no conversation within the coach, and hadn't been since the first few grumbles when Brandon boarded. The driver had walked the mules the first mile out of town to warm them up, then broke them into an easy lope to get them into their stride. Now the journey was rough with the coach jerking the occupants about. They hit a particularly vicious section of road and Brandon smacked his head against the wood behind him. This triggered off the pain in his right shoulder, the legacy of the late Chinaman. A wave of nausea swept through him and he clutched at the injury, biting back a yelp.

He didn't expect what happened next at all.

The elder of the women reached out to him and cupped his neck in her warm hand. When she spoke, it was in Spanish. 'You are in pain?' It was more of a statement than a question.

Although Brandon's knowledge of Spanish was basic, he knew enough to understand what she said, and replied in strained tones. 'Just something I picked up in Tombstone.'

'That is not the only thing,' she said, reverting to English. 'That lump on your forehead, also.'

Brandon gave her a weak smile. 'That's another story.'

She was bemused by the statement. 'When we get to our first stop, I have a medicine bag, and I will treat your injuries.'

Her companion adjusted her scarf and leaned forward. 'Karla, she is a *curandera,*' she said proudly. Seeing his frown, she went on to explain, 'She is a herb woman. Perhaps you know the word, *yarb?*'

'Ah, yes,' said Brandon.

'Karla will take very good care of you.

There is no injury that her potions cannot cure, and you will be in very safe hands with this wise one.'

'Thanks,' Brandon said. 'I appreciate your kindness, Karla.'

She gave him a dazzling smile and sat back, turned her mouth to her travelling companion's ear and spoke softly but quick, too quick for Brandon to pick up on what she was saying. The women broke into laughter, sharing some private joke. Brandon just hoped that it wasn't at his expense. He'd suffered too much over the last twelve hours.

He asked the younger girl, 'What is your name?'

'Maria Sanchez, *señor*,' she said. 'And yours?'

'James Brandon, at your service, *señorita.*'

She shook her head. '*Señora.*'

'Oh...' Disappointment registered on Brandon's face, and he heard the youngster give a slight groan. Evidently he must have been taking a keen interest in Maria and Karla. Brandon said, 'Are you on your way to Contention?'

Karla said, 'No and yes. We plan to catch the rail there and travel on to California.'

Brandon thought for a moment. 'California. There's a place I've never been to.'

'We have business in San Francisco,' Maria added.

'Ah … at least we will be travelling some of the journey together. I'm afraid that I must leave you both at Contention. There's some unfinished business that I've got to tend.'

The women nodded in unison.

The whip now urged the team into a canter, shaking the ancient mud wagon about on protesting springs. A silence fell inside the coach and Brandon moved back the canvas flap to look out into the night. He let the flap fall back into place and pulled up the collar of his jacket and settled back in his seat, trying to make himself as comfortable as he could.

The motion of the wagon and the gentle chatter of the women began to lull him into sleep. It wasn't long before his eyelids dropped and he began to doze.

Brandon felt himself being shaken awake. He cracked his eyes open, and saw Karla leaning forward, her hand on his knee.

'We are coming to the stage-station, *señor.*'

Brandon cleared his throat. 'Uh … *gracias.*' He smiled and received a dazzling one back. Karla lowered her eyes as the wagon came to a halt, the driver pulling on the binders nice and slowly.

Everyone in the coach was awake. The ugly cowboy tipped his hat back and ran a hand through his beard, taking in the other occupants with one sweeping glance. A voice from outside cut through the night air.

'Just put the whip down, and get out of the box.'

Brandon's brow furrowed in puzzlement, and he leaned across the youngster to pull back the flap. A rough hand caught him by his collar and jerked him back.

'What the…' he began. Suddenly he found

himself looking down the barrel of a revolver.

The cowboy grinned as he said, 'Don't you fret none, you goddamn' spic-lover. Just keep your nose inside.'

'I was looking...'

'I don't give a red cent!' bellowed the cowboy. 'Jus' don't interfere.'

Brandon hesitated, then said to the women in his halting Spanish, 'I think this is a hold-up, and that he's the inside man. If we do like they say, perhaps...'

'Quit jabberin' Mex!' The order came from the dude sitting next to him.

Brandon turned to face him, anger flushing his face. 'What the hell has it got to do with you?' he said.

'Plenty,' came the laconic reply as the dude pulled out a Colt Navy and thumbed back the hammer, the triple click sounding loud in the confines of the coach.

FIVE

Jim Brandon's heart sank. It might have been possible to take one of them on, but not two; especially since the dude now had his pistol pointing at the woman. Brandon thought that this was no ordinary hold-up. These men were either very professional or extremely cool characters. He realized that he had only heard one voice from outside, and hadn't heard the approach of horses. The stage had come to a gentle halt, not the jerking motion he would have expected with a surprise hold-up.

This was all too professional; even to the extent that the whip and the shotgun rider were involved.

The sumbitch dressed like a cowboy pushed himself up from the seat, adjusted his hat and looked fiercely at Brandon. 'Jus' stay put, mister,' he ordered.

Brandon returned the stare, but he had been on the receiving end of one too many bruises just lately to argue with the cowboy. He watched as the man threw open the door and jumped down.

The *curandera*, Karla said, 'We are being held up, no?'

Brandon nodded slowly. 'Seems that way, but don't let them frighten you. If all they want is money – give it to them.'

Maria Sanchez placed her hand across her breasts, hiding the gold locket hanging there. Brandon jerked his chin towards it. 'If they want that, don't hold back. There's plenty more they can do to you, apart from stealing that locket.'

Maria swallowed loudly, understanding exactly what he meant.

The tall dude stuck his gun into Brandon's ribs and said, 'When you've finished with the Messicans, lover-boy, get out of the coach nice and easy-like.'

'I'm warning you, I haven't got any

money,' Brandon lied.

'That's OK. Don't want anything from you anyway,' the dude said.

Brandon looked at him, puzzled.

A silence followed; then, 'Get out and stick your hands in the air.' The dude smiled, showing yellowed teeth.

Brandon turned to the women. 'Hang on in there.'

Karla shook her head. *'No entiendo.'*

The night air was cold. It bit into Brandon. He tugged at his Stetson, setting the hat lower, and pulled his collar up around his neck. The only light came from the stars and the small lantern hanging from the coach's boot. It shed a meagre glow across four faces.

Brandon recognized the driver, his shotgun guard and the cowboy who had snored his way from Tombstone to here, but the fourth man was unknown to him. His short-cropped white hair gleamed beneath his hat and he wore a crooked smile. There was something disturbingly vacant in his eyes as he lowered his rifle.

The stagecoach creaked and Brandon turned to watch the youngster emerge, gun drawn and aimed at him. Brandon cursed under his breath and realized that everyone inside the coach was involved. Then he thought that it may have been Behan's idea of revenge; to get him beyond Tombstone's limits and finish him off.

And as if to answer his question, the dude turned to the shotgun rider and said, 'There's only the two women left inside, Clancy.'

'OK.' The men stepped away from the driver and smiled. 'See, I told you that everything would be just dandy if you did as you were told.'

White spat on the ground. 'Yeah, we're all right up to now. But what you gonna do next?'

Le Duc chuckled, 'Wouldn't you like to know?'

'What *do* you want?' Brandon cut in.

Le Duc glanced at him. 'Shut your mouth.

When I want to hear from you, I'll let you know.'

Brandon felt the anger rising in him. His degradation in Tombstone had shortened his temper considerably, and now these bandits were making things worse for him. Obviously, the whip wouldn't be armed. Besides, two against five were long odds even at the best of times. He took a step nearer to Le Duc. 'Don't ever talk to me that way again, mister.'

Le Duc only laughed. 'You got some balls, feller.' He walked away shaking his head in disbelief, then he turned back to Brandon as he reached the coach door, cocked his head to one side and said, 'I wonder what it would be like to meet you under different circumstances.'

Brandon said, half-smiling, 'I wonder. Just me an' you?'

'Oh, yes.'

'Tell your boys to go away and I'll see if I can't oblige you.' Brandon was playing a bluff. His gun was in with his gear on top of the mud wagon. He just hoped that the gang-leader hadn't heard Behan tell everyone that.

Le Duc's big Smith & Wesson was back in the holster as he turned his back on Brandon once again. The gambler had every muscle tensed and he was quite ready to jump into action if the leader threw down on him.

But Clancy Le Duc only stepped up inside the stage and let out a low whistle. These were the prettiest two fillies he'd seen in quite some time, and they were his for the taking, if he had the mind to do so. There was something more important at hand, though, so he dismissed the thought as quickly as it formed.

He bowed to the ladies and said, '*Buenes tardes*. There's two ways we can do this. The hard way or the easy way. Which is it to be?'

Karla exchanged a look with Maria, then spoke to Le Duc. '*No entiendo.*'

'Ah … you don't understand me. I see.' He thought for a moment, then stuck his head out of the stage window. 'Hey, tough man. C'mere.'

Brandon turned to face him. 'You talkin' to me?'

Le Duc smiled. 'Yeah, I'm talkin' to you. You speak some Spanish, eh? Just translate what I tell you, and no extra bits thrown in. I speak a little of their tongue myself.'

Brandon shrugged and stepped closer to the wagon. Le Duc gave him the instructions; Maria was to remain in the wagon and her chaperon was to get out. All their personal belongings would remain on board. No funny stuff, otherwise folks would start getting hurt.

By the time he had finished translating for Le Duc, Jim Brandon had a fair idea what these bushwhackers were up to. But to voice it out aloud would probably mean certain death for him, Karla and the whip.

His eyes rose to Maria. They looked at each other. In the darkness of the wagon he could see her fear as plain as day. Then Le Duc was between them, saying to Brandon, 'Take this one and keep her by your side.'

He pulled Karla up from the seat by her slim wrist.

Brandon whispered quickly in her ear, 'Don't do anything foolish.'

Le Duc shot him an angry glare. 'What did you just say?'

'I told her not to be foolish.'

'That had better been all.'

'It was.'

Everyone apart from Maria Sanchez was out in the open. 'Lucky' Newbury and Ralph Burn leaned up against the boot. Bobby Hayes was dusting himself down and re-setting his hat. Davey Shaw was nervously fidgeting with his gloves. Only Clancy Le Duc was walking around like he had all the time in the world. He called the driver over to stand next to Brandon and Karla.

Le Duc said, 'You three had better keep quiet.' He turned and nodded to Burn. The white-haired man turned into the darkness and came back a moment later leading three horses, their muzzles wrapped in sacking.

'What're you gonna do with us?' Brandon asked.

Le Duc looked at him and said quickly. 'You're staying here and we're taking the coach and woman.'

White said, 'You ain't takin' *my* coach, mister.'

Le Duc smiled. 'You gonna stop me?'

'Damn' right I am.' And he stepped towards Le Duc.

The outlaw was too quick for the older man. He lashed out with a straight right jab that buried itself in White's beard. The Wells, Fargo coach driver staggered back and crashed down on his ass. Hayes and Newbury were smiling but their hands weren't far away from their pistols.

The whip shook his head and fought to get up. Brandon took him by the arms and pulled him up. Without a word, White shrugged the gambler away from him and went for Le Duc again.

Le Duc side-stepped the outstretched arms and planted a kick in White's stomach.

The old man doubled-up, breathing hard, not expecting the powerful uppercut to rock his head back. White landed heavily. The hard-packed earth did nothing to break his fall. He lay there, arms flung wide, not moving.

Brandon took Karla's hand from his forearm and bent to inspect the inert driver. He put a hand on the man's chest, feeling for a heartbeat. There was none. Then he felt at White's neck. No pulse.

Brandon straightened up and looked at Le Duc. 'He's dead. His heart must've given out.'

Le Duc smiled. 'Then there's one less of you to worry about.'

Brandon shook his head in disgust. 'You sorry bastard!'

Le Duc stood in front of Brandon. 'Listen, don't waste your worry on him. It's all over for the old man. But for you … it's just beginning.'

There was a puzzled look in Brandon's eyes. 'You care to explain that?'

'If it's all the same to you, I'll leave it to Mr Smith and Mr Wesson.'

The flame from the muzzle burnt the hair at his temple. Brandon gasped as though he had been struck and fell sideways. He landed hard on the manured road and did not move. The Mexican woman standing next to Brandon let out a shrill scream that was echoed by her companion, who was standing at the coach door.

Ralph Burn stepped out of the shadows and slapped Karla across the face with an open palm. The sound, as clear as a gun-shot, put an end to her screaming. Wearing a lop-sided grin, he turned to Maria, but she had balled her right fist into her mouth, stifling any more sounds.

Le Duc stood over Brandon and watched him breathing, his chest heaving with a wheezing sound. He could make out a line where the bullet had scored across his skull at the temple. The blood showed brown in the darkness, glimmering in the moonlight.

'He'll be all right,' Le Duc said. 'We'll

leave 'em here.' He turned to Karla and dug into his jacket pocket, pulling out a folded sheet of paper, yellowed with age. 'This here's a letter for your *patron, Señor* Eugenio Ramirez Sanchez. See that he gets it, iffen he wants to get his woman back. You understand me?' He thrust out the paper. *'Comprende usted?'* he repeated.

Karla's hand was shaking when she took the letter from the *gringo.* She hadn't understood all what he had said but knew from the tone of his voice that the letter meant something. She accepted it and nodded slightly, taking the sheet of paper in such a way as to avoid touching the man's fingers. The evil seemed to emanate from him.

Le Duc's voice was strong in the still of the night as he said 'OK, Raiders, mount up!'

Karla Luz did what she could for Jim Brandon. Working under the light of a quarter moon, she used a strip torn off from her petticoat to clean the blood off the head wound. Then, using water from the canteen that the youngest of the *bandidos* had left them, and dirt from the cold Arizona ground, she made up a mud paste which she applied to the wound, finally encasing Brandon's head in another strip of petticoat.

The man hadn't groaned or moved once as she nursed him. Karla worked quickly and skilfully but when she had finished she noticed the sweat was drying coldly in the night air, and shivered involuntarily, cursing the road agents for taking not only her herbs and potions with them, but her thick top-coat and spare undergarments as well.

Karla looked down at Brandon and sighed heavily. She hoped that he was a tough man. Without her herbs or any chicken entrails she knew that any poison would still be left in his injury. The mud paste would pull the torn skin together, but that was about all. It was up to the man himself to fight the fever that was building inside him. Again she cursed the men who did this.

Her mind turned to Maria – now left at the mercy of those men. Goodness knew what they would put her through. Karla fingered the note that the leader had given her, but although she could speak some little English, her knowledge of reading was very limited. There were one or two little words she could make out, but not enough to make sense of the letter.

She was also puzzled as to how the men knew of their travel route. It had been a closely-guarded secret with only her, Maria and *Señor* Sanchez holding the information of their planned route and mission. Somewhere along the line word had filtered out of their trip, and these men had been ready to capitalize on the information.

She sighed again and patted Brandon's fevered brow with a damp rag. Even in illness the man's face was ruggedly handsome. She smiled to herself as she remembered the attention he had paid to her in the coach. Normally men would prefer Maria to her. She knew that her charge was much more beautiful than she and younger, too. But this *gringo* had been interested in *her*, and that pleased her.

Karla was on the wrong side of thirty but knew she didn't look it. In fact, many took her and Maria for sisters, some said twins, although that was taking fancy too far. Before she died, her mother had passed on the secret to maintaining youthful looks, and Karla always took the medicine day in, day out.

But this feeling she had for the stranger at her feet, she had never experienced it before. Was it love? She shook her head at the very idea and quickly looked away, as though she expected his eyes to flicker open at any moment and catch her gazing at him, and see into her heart.

To take her mind off such fanciful thoughts, Karla busied herself in gathering wood to make up a small fire. With the box of lucifers taken from Brandon's jacket pocket, she lit the fire and watched it catch the kindle, then take a hold on the bigger sticks. The orange and red glow lit up the area immediately surrounding them and threw out a very welcome heat. Karla looked up into the night and guessed the time to be close to one or two o'clock. The stars were out and twinkling, the moon hung solid and silver and puffy clouds quickly scudded by. Across the land she heard the cries of nightbirds greeting each other, and the sharp howl of a lone coyote.

She moved Brandon as close to the fire as she dared and buttoned his jacket up to the throat. In the fire's glow his skin had grown redder as the fever took hold. Karla watched as one minute he groaned, the next he fell as still and silent as the grave.

There was nothing else she could do for him now – except pray.

It must have been close to three o'clock when a sound disturbed her fitful sleep. Karla didn't know when she had fallen asleep, but she woke up next to Brandon, the closeness of his body keeping her warm. The fire had all but died out. She strained her ears for the sound but there was nothing. A cricket chirped nearby and a mate echoed the sound a ways off.

She held her breath and waited. She could make out the shape of the land, the rising hills and trees and the light from the moon spreading its pale shine across the ground. Then the noise came again.

She counted to herself in the silence, then stood up. She stepped back and moved a good few feet away from the restless body of Jim Brandon. The noise was coming closer, off to her right, and Karla moved into the shadows of a rocky outcrop. She felt the fear rising in her, tightening her throat, but thinking about Maria and those men helped her overcome this initial onslaught of terror.

She stopped and pressed her body against a large boulder, almost willing herself to be moulded into its shape. Her breathing was under control and her eyes were wide as she peered through the night gloom, past the small fire and Brandon, and in the direction of the approaching noise.

The squeaking from a dry rear wheel-axle ground against the night's silence, growing louder as it came near. Karla could make out the black silhouette of a wagon heading straight for their camp fire.

There were no details that she could make out, but the wagon rolled laboriously on, stopping only when it was a few yards away. A deep, booming male voice cut the air, startling her.

'Hello, the camp,' it sang out.

The *curandera* remained silent. Waiting. She heard the wagon creak as the man moved. Karla felt the panic rising in her. She didn't know whether the newcomer was armed or not. Was he dangerous? Could she trust him?

'Anyone there?' the voice called out.

Karla moved slightly, her toe touching against a rock. Slowly and carefully, she bent down and felt it. It was bigger than her fist, and when she lifted it, it was reassuringly heavy. She stood up again, looking towards the wagon.

She must have made more noise than she thought, because the stranger with the wagon was nowhere in sight now. Karla moved away from the rock and looked over at Brandon. The man was still in feverish sleep. As she turned, she saw a flicker of movement from the corner of her eye. She brought her right hand up, the one with the rock in it, to show she wasn't afraid.

'That's far enough.' The voice came from behind her.

Karla stopped in her tracks.

'I don't know what you've got in your hand, but whatever it is, you'd better drop it.'

With her hand still raised, Karla said, *'Quienes? Que quiere usted?'*

'Uh...' He was momentarily flustered. Then spoke in broken Spanish. 'Put whatever it is you've got in your hand down. Then turn to face me. Slowly, like.'

Karla said. 'It is only a rock, *señor.*'

'Like I said, put it down.'

'Si, señor.' Karla lowered her arm and dropped the rock, turning to face the man as she did so.

He moved out of the shadows, from almost the exact spot in front of her. There was nothing menacing about the tall man as the firelight threw relief on to his face. He wasn't even armed, he just stood there with his hands held together in front of him.

Karla was surprised. The man was dressed in black broadcloth, with a starched white collar at his throat – a man of God!

'Forgive me, father, I did not know…'

'There is nothing to forgive, my child.' His voice was deep but reassuringly so. 'But what has happened here? Are these men dead?'

Karla said, 'The old one is, but the younger man is still alive, though in a bad way.'

'What happened?'

Karla told him of the events of the stagecoach hold-up, the killing of the Wells, Fargo driver, of Brandon's shooting and the kidnapping of her ward. All the while, the reverend remained silent, his eyes concentrating on Karla's face.

'I've done all I can for him,' she concluded. 'But without my herbs, I am not sure the wound will heal correctly.'

The preacher moved towards her and took her by the arm, gently guiding her back towards the fire. They stopped and he squatted down, examining Brandon.

'You've done a good job,' he said, then stood. 'I reckon that he'll live.'

'I hope so,' she muttered.

A silence followed. Then, 'Come with me to the wagon. I've got supplies that we could use – coffee, bacon and such. Perhaps something that you can wear to protect you from the cold.' He smiled and held out his hand.

It wasn't long before Karla sat with a fleece-lined leather coat draped around her shoulders, and her stomach full with bacon, beans and strong coffee. She watched the preacher until he had finished his own coffee, then said, 'What is your name?'

'Reverend Joshua Slate,' he replied. 'But you can call me Joe.'

'What are you doing out here, in the middle of the night … Joe?'

Slate said, 'I do my best thinking at night. My mule's got a good sense of direction, so I let her lead me wherever she wants to go.'

Karla nodded. 'It is a good thing that you and your burro found us. I wouldn't have known what to do with him in the morning.' She looked across at Brandon.

Slate stretched his long legs out in front of him. 'Well, now, I reckon you should get a good night's sleep. Come sun-up, we can both take care of that problem. There's a mattress in the back of the wagon. You're welcome to use that.'

'But where…?'

Slate held up a hand to stop her. 'Don't worry about me, lady. I've slept on solid ground more times than I care to recall. Now you go and get your head down. There ain't no sense in both of us being awake all night.'

Karla smiled. *'Muchas gracias, Señor* Slate.'

''nada, señorita.'

Slate watched Karla climb in back of the wagon, then lay down on his side so that he could see both the man and the lovely Mexican lady. It was in his mind to bury the old man in the morning, early, before the sun rose and began to bake the ground. After that he could set about getting these people to a doctor. Karla had mentioned that Tombstone wasn't far, perhaps fifteen or twenty miles.

But for now he, too, was plumb tuckered. He snuggled up closer to the fire, watching the flames lick at the dry wood, making an occasional crack beneath the bigger logs and sending sparks up into the air. He thought of the bottle of mescal tucked behind his seat on the wagon but shrugged. He'd gotten himself nice and comfortable now, and couldn't be bothered to move.

SIX

A faint breeze came off the hills, pushing dust and grey embers over Slate's face. He came awake with a start, propping himself up on one elbow and cracking his sleep-encrusted eyes open. He looked over the camp. He was the only one awake and the wind was the only thing moving.

The rising sun was hidden by thick grey clouds. A few stars still dotted the sky. Slate knew that it was time to get that grave dug. From what Karla had told him, he would have no other choice but to get her and the man to safety, then go after the gang of cutthroats who'd caused all this upset before their trail went cold.

He stood up, yawned and stretched, then set about getting the fire going again. He struck a match with his thumbnail and watched the kindling catch. With that chore completed, he set to his other task, removing a long handled spade tied to the side of the wagon. Slate walked over to a patch of ground near a bush of mesquite and began to dig.

He was aching from the digging when Karla approached, carrying a cup of hot coffee and a tin plate of food. He rubbed at the small of his back and showed no surprise at seeing her.

She smiled. 'Here, you need to rest.'

He nodded. 'I reckon I've dug enough to cover him. The sun'll be burning the ground soon, so we'd best get him in before he starts stinking the place up.'

Karla smiled faintly. 'You seem to take everything so … so casually.'

'Yeah, I s'pose I do. But I've seen and done most things in my life, *señorita,* a few things that I didn't ought to have done, too. These days, though, I reckon I've found my calling, so I take things one day at a time. This land's too rough with a body to plan too far into the future.'

'I understand.' She offered him the cup and plate, and turned away.

Slate was left standing by the mesquite bush, a look of amusement on his face. He watched her bend over Brandon, untie the petticoat bandage and examine the mud paste. She was pleased that it hadn't cracked with all his thrashing about. She replaced the bandage and wet a piece of cloth, washing Brandon's face with great care.

Slate watched this as he sat and ate. He knew that there must be more to this lady and her caring of the man than met the eye, but it wasn't his business and he remained silent as he finished the food.

Jethro White was buried at six in the morning, with the preacher saying a few words over his body. A crude wooden cross was placed at the head of the grave. Joshua Slate and Karla Luz were his only mourners on that warm August morning.

Karla sat against the front wheel of the wagon, her legs straight out in front of her, resting on the hard-packed dirt floor, drinking a cup of brackish water. The sun was rising and the land was heating up. The breeze that had woken Slate was gone now and she fanned herself with her free hand.

Slate was tending to his mule, his back to her. She thought of the tall preacher and gave a small smile. It was strange that he should have appeared in the middle of the night, just when she needed him. She looked at Slate whilst he had dug the grave, without him knowing it. She guessed his age at around forty. He had blond hair turning grey at the temples, and hard blue eyes – not the sort that looked at you, but *into* you. He was heavy, thick in the chest and shoulders, but evidently his age hadn't slowed him down.

Now he had finished with the mule and was turning to faced her. Karla dropped her eyes, pretending to be asleep. Slate's voice was soft. 'Karla. Karla, wake up.'

She looked up at him.

Slate said, 'It's time to be moving on.'

Karla nodded. 'We will have to put *Señor*

Brandon on the mattress, and I will travel up front with you, Reverend Slate,' she said.

Slate agreed. 'Right, but call me Joe, will you?'

The mule pulled the wagon along with an easy strength, and they travelled across the rough terrain without too much worry. Karla had shed the leather coat and rocked on the hard wooden seat next to Slate. The preacher handled the wagon without any trouble, his eyes constantly scanning the land around them. Beyond the brush there were pinon pines on the hills stretching away on either side of them. Every so often, Karla looked around at Brandon, checking to make sure he was all right. He was.

Slate broke the silence. 'Karla, thinking back on the hold-up ... was there anything those men said about why they were taking your ward hostage?'

Karla thought for a moment, then remembered the letter she had been given. She dug the paper out and gave it to Slate. He read it slowly and gave a low whistle.

'Ten thousand dollars?'

Karla said. 'What for?'

'You mean you haven't read this?'

'I can't read – English, that is.'

'It seems those fellers have taken *Señora* Sanchez to get ten thousand dollars out of her old man. He must be rich.'

'He is.'

Slate arched an eyebrow.

Karla said, '*Señor* Sanchez is a diamond merchant in Mexico, worth much *dinero*.'

'I see.' Slate thought for a while. 'But what were you two ladies doing so far away from home?'

'We were on our way to catch the rail to San Francisco. *Señor* Sanchez thought it would be safer to travel by way of Contention than by some other more direct route to California.'

'Why?'

Karla shrugged. 'Perhaps he feared for our safety.'

Slate shook his head. 'He couldn't have cared that much, otherwise he would have sent some men with you.'

'Do you think that *Señor* Sanchez does not care, he does. But there is something that you do not know.'

'Oh, and what's that?'

It was Karla's turn to shake her head. 'I cannot tell you.'

Slate shot her a glance. Karla's mouth was thin-lipped.

'So, that's all I'm getting out of you, is it?' he asked.

'Si, señor.'

Slate thought, it's back to *señor* now. I must have blundered into something touchy. Then he got to thinking if Jim Brandon had anything to do with the women. Had he been sent along to protect them without their knowing it? Maybe, but he wasn't going to get any more answers out of Karla right now.

'Everything comes to he who waits,' he muttered softly.

They rode into a canyon at mid-afternoon. The mule was lathered up and Slate decided to call a halt. Karla took the opportunity to check on Brandon. His fever had broken and now his breathing was more regular. His face was gaunt, his cheeks sunken and dark circles had appeared under his eyes, but his heartbeat was stronger and more rhythmic. She was pleased at his progress, and her smile showed her relief. She jumped down from the back of the wagon and walked over to a clump of mesquite, ready to gather some firewood. Slate's voice stopped her.

'This is a cold camp, Karla.'

She looked at him, surprise in her eyes.

'Nothing's wrong,' Slate said. 'But we haven't been following the trail back to Tombstone.'

'Why not?'

'If we did, then them fellers would get clean away. We just don't have the time to double-back on ourselves. I figured it would be better to cut their trail and find out where they're holed up. Then you can get us some help.'

She frowned. 'You don't sound like a preacher now.'

'Like I told you, I've done a few things in the past. But we're not getting into that now. The important thing is that we've got to keep up with those men.' He paused for a minute then said, 'I know we ain't travelling fast, but if we keep up a goodly pace, then I'm sure we'll come across a homestead or the like. I'll leave you and your man-friend there and go after these kidnappers on my own.'

'But there's five, maybe six of them, and only one of you.'

'Make that two.'

Slate and Karla turned around and gaped at Jim Brandon, who was sitting up in the wagon, watching them.

'Oh, *señor!*' Karla moved away from Slate and rushed towards the wagon. 'Are you all right?'

He rubbed his head. '*Quien sabe?* Who is to say?'

Karla looked at him, wondering if the bullet had done some damage to his brain, and hoping that it hadn't. She smiled at him.

Brandon said, 'Keep doing that, and I'll be OK.'

'You look thinner,' Karla said. 'And a shade paler, too.'

'I'm none too surprised, are you?' he replied. He looked over to Slate. 'Who are you? A preacher?'

'That's right. The name's Joshua Slate.' Slate moved forward and offered Brandon his hand.

Brandon accepted it and said, 'I'm obliged for all your help, reverend.'

'Call me Joe. And it wasn't all my doing. This here young *señorita* has been looking after you. I only drove the wagon.'

Brandon nodded. 'Sure. But I just overheard you planning to take on those hardcases on your own, didn't I? I don't think you know what you're up against.'

'To tell you the truth, Brandon, neither do I, but I won't let it worry me none.'

'You're a different kind of preacher than any I've met before,' Brandon said.

'Like I've been telling Karla, I've been

around. Not everyone is born a preacher, and I surely didn't start my days as one.'

Brandon brought himself upright, pulling a revolver into sight. Karla gasped, but Slate remained calm.

Brandon said, 'I see you travel armed, Slate.'

He smiled. 'You never know when you're going to need a little help in this world, Brandon.'

Brandon nodded his agreement. 'Don't suppose there's any grub or coffee around, is there?'

''Fraid not – it's a cold camp,' Slate said.

'What are you going to do?' Karla asked Brandon.

'The reverend answered that,' Brandon replied. 'We go after them.'

'*We?*' echoed Slate.

'Hell – beg your pardon – you don't think that you're going up against five heavily-armed men on your own, do you?'

Slate said, 'You ain't exactly in good shape to render me much assistance, are you?'

Brandon brushed that point aside. 'It's just a graze, that's all. I've been in worse scraps.'

Karla touched his shoulder and said, 'Let me have a look at that graze, then.'

As Karla re-examined the wound, Brandon looked off into the distance, thinking; trying to weigh up the odds and coming out with a tangled mess of deuces. Those bandits were clever. They'd captured the stagecoach somewhere outside of Tombstone, then rode it into town and only allowed Karla and Maria on to it. He, Brandon, had come on board at the last moment, and they'd obviously been unable to argue with Sheriff Behan about it. They even had the gall to keep the old driver with them to make it look authentic. That took some courage to pull off.

Now he and this preacher were planning on going up against them with nothing but a clapped-out wagon pulled by a mangy-looking mule and one Colt .45 between them. That was what he called stacked odds. He patted his jacket pocket and breathed a sigh of relief that what was left to his bankroll was still in place.

Brandon looked at Karla. Their eyes met. In that one look a thousand unspoken words passed between them. Slate recognized the look and turned away.

'In case you're wondering,' Slate said, breaking the spell, 'there's a rifle and another Colt stowed away behind the seat.'

Slate never ceased to amaze Brandon. He reached under the oilcloth and brought out the Winchester and Colt. They were both in prime condition and he ran a hand over them, feeling the thin film of oil on their surfaces. He looked up at Slate.

'T'ain't no use letting them rust,' Slate said. 'You never know when they're going to be needed.'

Brandon looked at him quickly, respect showing on his face, and said, 'That's true enough. Now, how about telling me your plan? How're we going to go after them?'

Slate grinned. 'Firstly, we got to get Karla to safety. She'll have to telegraph *Señor*

Sanchez and tell him what's happened.'

Brandon said, 'That means she'll have to go to Tombstone.'

'That's right.'

'There's one problem.'

'What's that?' asked Karla.

Brandon said, 'I had a run-in with the law back there, and they warned me out of town.' He turned to Karla. 'That's what all the trouble was about when I boarded. I don't think luck's running my way just now, so *I* can't risk it going back.'

Slate thought for a moment then said, 'We'll have to stick with my original idea of getting to a settlement, then. There we can get us some fresh mounts, then Karla can take my wagon an' wire Sanchez. In the meanwhile, you and I'll follow their trail.'

Brandon got down from the wagon, a little uneasy on his feet. 'Is that it? Your plan?'

Slate nodded. 'So far.'

'So far, so good, then. Let's get moving.'

Karla looked puzzled and moved next to Brandon.

'Don't worry,' Brandon said. 'Everything's going to work out fine. We'll get Maria back, just you wait and see.'

Karla reached out and touched Brandon's face with her fingertips, running them gently down his cheek, feeling the roughness of a day's growth of whiskers. Brandon smiled at her and removed her hand, holding it in his for a moment and squeezing it gently.

'OK, you love-birds,' Slate interrupted. 'Let's get moving.'

Brandon shot him an angry glare, but Slate ignored it, saying instead, 'Could be my lucky day, running into you two. I ain't officiated at a wedding since I can't remember when.'

Lucky Newbury wasn't feeling so lucky. Davey Shaw's first punch caught the outlaw squarely in the mouth, splitting his bottom lip wide open. Newbury staggered back against the rock face, mouth open, blood splashing his beard.

Shaw stood over him, the knuckles of his

right hand red and sore. He wasn't gong to wait for Newbury to recover. Newbury had provoked the fight; he was there to carry it through.

Newbury brought his bloodied fingers away from the cut lip, looked down at the blood and said, 'All right, Shaw! You want a fight over the Messican whore, I'll give you one!'

'I'm just telling you is all, Newbury. Don't call her a whore.'

'Jeez, kid. You treat her like she's royalty.'

'I don't, but even so, you got no right to keep calling her names.'

'Any woman's a whore who'd as soon spread her legs as do an honest day's toil.'

Shaking with rage, Shaw glared back at Newbury. The bearded man had been ogling the woman ever since they'd reached camp. His lewd suggestions to Maria disgusted Shaw; Newbury had even made a grab for her once, but had been warned off by Le Duc. Now, with the boss-man away with Ralph Burn, taking care of the unwanted stagecoach, there was no stopping him. He had groped at Maria's breasts and that was when Davey Shaw had seen red, and thrown the first punch.

Newbury spat out blood, collected himself and lunged away from the wall. Side-stepping, Shaw slammed a punch to the side of Newbury's face and quickly followed it with a sharp jab to his kidney. Newbury staggered but turned to smash a back-handed blow at Shaw, which connected with his right cheekbone.

Shaw's legs buckled, and his knees gave way.

Newbury saw his opening and was upon him, throwing hard punches to his head. Shaw fell, and instinctively rolled under the horses picketed between the pine trees, as Newbury tried to stomp him with his spurs. Shaw came up on his knees, dazed and fighting for breath; everything around him was slightly fuzzy. But he didn't fail to see Newbury pushing his way through the horses, following him.

Shaw stood up and drove a knee into Newbury's gut as the man rushed him. The bow-legged outlaw was lifted off his feet. Shaw kneed him in the face while he was bent over, and Newbury collapsed on his back.

'C'mon, Lucky,' Bobby Hayes called out. 'You ain't gonna let that little pisser beat you now, are you?'

Shaw turned and gave him a fierce look.

Hayes just smiled back.

Lucky shook his head like a wounded animal, blood dribbling from his nose and mouth, then charged at Shaw. The youngster ducked underneath his outstretched arms and banged a fist into Newbury's bruised gut. The little man's frame shook but he wasn't finished. Gulping in air loudly through his mouth, he brought both hands down and grabbed a handful of Shaw's hair and yanked his head back. Then, standing on tiptoes, he head-butted Shaw in the face, busting his nose.

Davey Shaw gasped and staggered back.

He knew that he wouldn't be able to keep the stronger man at bay for much longer. Tears stung his eyes and his breathing was becoming laboured, but he realized that he had to go on, more to prove something to himself than anything else. He saw Newbury taking a wild swing at his head, ducked and brought up a double-handed fist under Newbury's jaw, rocking his head back. He followed it with a fusillade of body blows, loosening up the other outlaw.

Newbury suffered the blows in a series of grunts, letting the younger man use up more of his energy with the body blows which he was well capable of taking, and waiting until he was backed up against a tree. Then he drove into his counter-attack. He hammered the boy with a left to the jaw, a right to the stomach, then a fearsome uppercut that sent Shaw sprawling onto his back.

Newbury stepped over the youngster, blood dropping off his beard and spattering the boy's shirt-front. 'Any time you want a fight,' he said breathlessly, 'I'll oblige yer.'

Shaw looked up at him with dazed eyes. 'It ain't over yet.'

Newbury frowned. 'What?'

There was no need for Shaw to answer him. He brought his legs up in a blur, catching Newbury in the crotch with the heels of his boots. The bearded outlaw screamed like a stuck pig and held his manhood for all it was worth. Shaw scrambled up again and measured up to Newbury; standing to his full height, and using all of his remaining strength, he hammered a right-handed swing into Newbury's ugly face.

Newbury fell back, crashing down on to his butt. His head was ringing and lights danced before his eyes. He groaned as the fall sent fresh pain raging between his legs. He wanted to puke. He looked up. Shaw was standing unsteadily on his feet, his right eye already discoloured and swollen, almost half-closed.

'I'll kill you,' he muttered, and reached for the tied-down pistol on his right thigh.

A lariat dropped over his head and shoulders, tightened and pinned his arms against his sides before he could complete the draw. He turned his groggy head, and saw Le Duc sitting easily in his saddle, the end of the rope tied around his saddlehorn.

'You trying to tell everyone where we are?' Le Duc asked mildly.

'No,' Newbury replied, puzzled.

Le Duc grunted. 'Fire that pistol and that's exactly what you'll do.' He stepped down, walking towards Newbury and bringing in the lariat. 'I ain't been gone for more'n a hour, and I have to come back to all this.' He waved a hand at the two fighters, then continued, 'What the hell's been happening?'

Newbury met his eyes and spat blood on the ground. 'Hold on, Clance. That youngster started all...'

'Go to hell, Newbury!' Shaw snorted.

Le Duc removed the lasso and finished recoiling it, saying, 'Put up the pistol, Lucky. You ain't gonna shoot the boy, or no one else, come to that.'

Newbury's face reddened and he took his hand off the revolver's butt. He remained silent, getting his breath back, thinking about what had happened to John Franklin, how easily Le Duc had dealt with him. He wasn't in Franklin's class, not by any means, so he let it set awhile, then said, 'Listen, I … er … we didn't mean no real harm. I just wanted a bit of fun, that's all.'

'That's right, Clancy,' Bobby Hayes said, backing his fellow outlaw. 'Just a bit of fun is all.'

Le Duc eyed him from beneath the brim of his hat, then sighed, realizing what all the commotion had really been about. He finished fastening the rope to his saddle, then turned to face Newbury and Shaw. He took off his hat and ran a hand through his greasy hair, thinking, then crammed the hat back on his head and said to Newbury, 'I'll tell you this just the once. Keep your peter to yourself. That woman is our ticket out of this place, and if for one moment you or anybody else is gonna jigger the deal, they'll have to answer to me. D'you understand?'

Newbury bobbed his head.

Le Duc looked at the others, watched and heard them agree, then smiled. 'Now that we've got *that* good an' clear, let's have us something to eat.' He turned to Maria. 'Make yourself useful, girl. Get to fixin' us some coffee and food, savvy?'

Maria slowly shook her head.

'Don't play dumb with me,' snarled Le Duc. 'You don't cook, you don't eat – it's as simple as that. *Comprende?*'

The woman nodded her head, gathered her long skirt in both hands and moved over to the campfire, casting a concerned look at Davey Shaw's battered face. The youngster watched her, feeling his face redden still further as their eyes met.

Ralph Burn laughed. 'I swear that boy's got eyes as big as a love-sick cow!'

Le Duc smiled. 'Knock it off, Ralph. Just let's get this thing over and done with, and stop ribbing the boy. We're stuck with her for the better part of a week, maybe two, so let's keep things nice an' easy between us all, eh?'

The atole Maria prepared was passable. Although only Lucky complained about the flour gruel, the other men ate without complaint. Rarely did their diet differ from steak and potatoes to potatoes and steak. The coffee was good, though; fresh and strong enough to float a bullet in.

Once fed and watered, the men lazed about the camp, sitting in the shade of the main tent, rolling smokes or just drifting off to sleep. Le Duc had posted Bobby Hayes on the look-out rock which covered the narrow defile leading up the treacherous mountain path that led to their hide-out. It was an ideal place for the camp because the defile was the only way in or out. Nature had provided them with a good cover of scrub oak and pines, and a water supply only yards away. Le Duc claimed to have discovered the place when a band of ragheads had chased him and a previous partner after they had stolen back a few mules and cows.

Since that run-in with the Apaches about four years earlier, Le Duc had used the hide-away on a regular basis. He had never found a better location from which to operate his nefarious activities. But now Le Duc felt exhausted. The days of tension prior to the kidnapping were being released like the cracking of a bullwhip, and with the act done, he felt drained. Checking over his men and their beautiful prisoner, he sighed heavily, then strode off to his own tent. It was set aside from the other, pitched with its rear against the rock face, a position with which he felt safe.

Davey Shaw watched Le Duc pull the tent flap shut behind him, then looked over to Maria. He had to wait a minute before she looked up from the fire. When at last he had her attention, he signalled with a nod that she should come and join him.

Maria looked at the youngster's battered face. His eye was completely closed by the swelling, and coloured a vicious purple. She wondered what he wanted. She cast a nervous glance at Newbury. He had his chin slumped on his chest and his breathing was ragged as he slept. She hoped that he would live the rest of his life in pain. Then she looked back at Shaw and gave a slight nod.

She stood up with two mugs of coffee and walked over to where Shaw sat with his back against a boulder, shaded by a big pine. Shaw took his mug and asked Maria to sit with him. They drank in silence. Maria sensed that he had something to tell her, or ask her, but either way he just couldn't find the appropriate words.

Maria took the initiative, speaking in English, 'Thank you, *señor.* For defending my honour.'

Shaw blushed as he sipped his coffee. 'No problem. I had to do it.'

'Why?'

'It's what my pa taught me. You never bad-mouth a woman.'

Maria looked at him. 'Your father was a good man, *si?*'

Shaw gave a little laugh. 'Heck, no. He was

a bad ’un, through an’ through. But he wouldn’t have no woman insulted in front of him.’

‘Then he was a good man, despite his wrong-doings.’ She paused to drink her coffee, then went on, ‘But I cannot explain to myself why you need to ride with these *bandidos.* Surely there must be something else you can do?’

Shaw shook his head. ‘Uh-huh. I ain’t but seventeen, an’ I spent most of my time nursemaiding my ma and two younger sisters. My pa rode for Le Duc ’til he got kilt. With the money he earned, he set us up on a small ranch, but when he died there was no more money coming in, and ma was frantic about the money she owed. So I robbed a store, and would have got caught if it hadn’t been for Le Duc. Roping in with him seemed the easiest way to get us out of trouble.’

‘But stealing and killing isn’t easy, is it?’

‘I know,’ he said miserably.

Maria sighed and she felt a wave of sympathy for the boy. Maria had never known poverty in her life. She had never felt the cold pang of hunger, or had to worry where the next *centavo* was going to come from. She was the wife of an extremely wealthy diamond merchant.

She said, 'Why don't you go back to your family? They would understand.'

He shook his head again. 'You think I can just up an' go? Well, sorry ma'am, it don't work that way.'

'What are they planning to do with me?'

Shaw detected the slight tremor in Maria's voice and was undecided as to whether or not to tell her the truth. He decided to be honest for once. 'Le Duc has written a ransom note to your old man. Ten thousand dollars in exchange for your safe return.'

Maria lifted the mug to her lips, thinking, then said, 'My husband, he will pay.'

'That's what Le Duc figured.'

'And then he will have you hunted down, and killed one by one.'

Shaw glanced at Maria, wondering if she

was trying to frighten him. Either way, her words unsettled him, and he drained the rest of his coffee in one gulp, wiping the spillage with the back of his hand.

'*Lo siento,*' she said. 'I am sorry. I did not mean to make you afraid, but I only say the truth. My husband, he is extremely rich and powerful. I am sure *Señor* Le Duc knows this. But what he does not know is that my husband is also insanely jealous. If he ever thought, even for one minute, that I had been … molested or harmed in any way, he would not hesitate in turning over every rock in Arizona to find the men responsible.'

Davey Shaw's heart was pounding. He'd never been so confused before. He scratched his head, worrying about his mixed-up feelings. On the one hand he owed his allegiance to Le Duc himself, not to the Raiders. His pa had trusted his well-being to Le Duc, and the top-hand had sworn to take care of the boy. He'd even gunned down his right-hand man as a result of what had started as an argument between Franklin and Shaw.

But now Shaw was in conflict with his own feelings. He toyed with the coffee mug, rolling it between his palms, thinking. Maria Sanchez placed her hand softly on his forearm. Goosebumps arose, and he looked at her.

She said, 'The time has come for you to make a decision. There is only one right road to take, but you must decide for yourself. You either intend to spend the rest of your life amongst these *bandidos*...'

'Or?'

'Or leave them and go your own way. To become your own man.'

Davey chewed on that for a minute, then said, 'If I go, you gotta come with me.'

'No, you must go alone. I would only slow you down.'

'Uh-uh. When I leave, you're coming with me,' Shaw insisted.

Maria sighed and smiled across at Shaw. '*Si*, but I am not a very good rider. I doubt I would be able to keep up with you.'

Shaw shrugged. 'We'll sort something out.'

But already the seeds of doubt were growing in the back of Maria's mind. She wondered whether she had actually persuaded the boy to meet an early death. The thought made her skin grow clammy, and she shuddered involuntarily. Shutting her eyes did nothing to keep out the image of Shaw stretched out on the ground, his body riddled with blackened bullet holes, gaping open-mouthed as he lay dying, and Le Duc standing over him, hands on hips, laughing.

Shaw must have sensed her unease, because he touched her hand and said, 'Don't fret, Maria. Things'll work out just dandy, you'll see.' Then he whispered to himself, 'I hope.'

SEVEN

Adjusting the set of his hat-brim, Joshua Slate looked around. The ranch was now just a dot on the horizon.

Jim Brandon had lapsed into silence after a couple of miles. His head pounded under the intense heat, and his eyes ached. Reverend Slate held the reins of the claybank loose in his left hand, his right holding a Winchester across his lap. It was a position he found comfortable. The land was unfamiliar to him, as it was to Brandon, and he pushed the claybank northwest, up towards higher ground.

Brandon was quiet and drowsy by midday. His head still ached but the powders that the Whiteheads had supplied him with had taken away a great deal of the pain. He found himself wondering about their next move. It seemed simple; to find Maria Sanchez' abductors and rescue her from them. But it wasn't quite that simple for him. He was no tracker, not even any great shakes with a sidearm. The unfamiliar weight of a holster tied down on his right thigh was uncomfortable. He was happier with his shoulder rig and the snub-barrelled Lightning he'd adopted when he first embarked upon his card-playing career. Now he found that he was having to depend on the reverend to see him through this one, and thought that he might have acted too hastily in setting himself up as knight errant.

Slate, Brandon and Karla had followed the dirt road until they came across a small farm. The Whiteheads, a childless couple in their late forties who earned a crust by keeping livestock, fed and watered the trio, sold Slate the claybank and Brandon the big grey. They agreed to look after Karla, and promised that they would see her safely to Tombstone, so that she could wire *Señor* Sanchez. Brandon and Slate rode out later that morning, the sun burning fiercely out of a cloudless sky, leaving Karla alone on the stoop, her hand raised in farewell.

Brandon looked over to Slate, noting the easy way he rode. 'Hey, Reverend. Can I ask you something?'

'What's that, my son? And like I said…'

'I know, I know. The name's Joe.' He paused a moment. 'You ride pretty good for a sky pilot.'

'What's that got to do with anything?'

Brandon grinned. 'OK. I'll say what's on my mind. I just got me a feeling that you were cavalry once.'

Slate looked across at his companion. A vein stood out on his forehead, throbbing. Brandon knew that it wasn't the done thing to pry into a man's past, but he had to know if he was going to get out of this one intact.

'Well, now, you seem to have me pegged,' Slate allowed after a while.

There was a long silence between them. Brandon watched Slate from the corner of his eye. The preacher chewed on his top lip as he deliberated the point. Before Jim Brandon could say anything else, Slate brought the claybank to a halt.

'OK, Jim,' he said looking the gambler in the eye. 'This is the first and only time you'll hear this. Yeah, I was cavalry. Rode for the Union, under Colonel Minty. We were the best cavalry outfit the Union had. They called us "The Sabre Brigade".' He removed his hat and mopped his sweat-speckled brow with his jacket-sleeve. 'Back in sixty-three we were heading for Lebanon, pursuing John Morgan's Raiders. But when we got there they'd skedaddled, so Minty ordered us to push on after 'em.

'I had a good friend named Tom Mills. We grew up together, an' all that stuff. We always watched over each other, and when we skirmished with Morgan some fifteen hours later, Tom saved my life. Well, to cut a long story short, we came under artillery fire sometime later and Tom got hisself blown apart.

'My mind went kinda weird after that, an'

I didn't know which way to turn. We were being attacked from every which way, and it went on till darkness fell. Then Minty done something I'd never believed would've happened – he ordered our retreat. To a man we'd vowed never to surrender. When it was pitch black we made our way close to the Spring Creek bridge. The Feds, though, they'd burnt it down, so the colonel had to take us on a dirt road and up through rocks and dense stands of cedar. None of us had slept for more'n twenty-four hours, and I guess I must've fallen asleep in the saddle.

'Well, the next thing I knew I was waking up with a lump the size of an apple on my head. My horse was gone and so were the Fourth Mich. All I had was my sabre and a brace of Remingtons. There I was in some Godforsaken place with no food or water and the Feds coming up behind me. I must've stumbled through the night for more'n a couple of miles before I heard the Feds a little way off. So I concealed myself in the undergrowth.

'There must've been more'n a thousand men after old Minty, and considering the state my regiment was in, I guessed that it wouldn't be too long before they got caught. I asked myself what was I going to do now. I couldn't catch up with the Fourth, and I sure wasn't going back the way I'd just come. So I walked, and walked, not coming across man, beast nor water for nigh on four days. Then I woke up in an abandoned, rat-infested cabin, and felt like hell on a pair of legs. Must've lost ten or more pounds, and half my mind to boot.

'All I kept seeing was Tom's body being ripped apart in my mind's eye. I realized that there had to be more to this life than dying. That we'd been put on this earth for some greater reason. Anyway, there was this dog-eared Bible someone had left behind, and I began to read it. Jim, I'll tell you that I've never been so comforted as when I read those words.

'It took a while for me to get my body back into shape, but the Bible had healed my mind. When I stepped out of the cabin it was like I had been reborn. Think about it; the cavalry must've posted me as dead, I was in a new land and felt like a new man. I could start my life over again and devote my time in spreading the good word. Now, I don't preach to those who don't want to listen, and over the last seventeen years I've pleased myself as to where I go and who I talk to.'

Brandon said, 'It looks as if the Good Book lived up to its name.'

'It did for me.'

'My ma used to read it to us sometimes, and drag us off to Sunday meetings. Thinking back, seems it was all fire 'n' brimstone, like the preacher wanted to scare the hell outta us.'

Slate grinned. 'Yeah, you'll always get that sort. Give us good preachers a bad name.'

Brandon wondered if Slate was a good preacher or not, then thought that seventeen years was a long time to spend just riding around without any particular aim.

So he voiced his thought. 'You must have something in mind. Something special you want to achieve in life, rev … uh … Joe?'

'What d'you mean?'

Suspicion had crept into Slate's voice, but Brandon ignored it. 'I mean, you don't strike me as a body to spend the rest of his days just wandering.'

'The Lord Jesus Christ did.'

'That was only for forty days and nights, I seem to recollect.'

'Yeah, but His wanderings in the wilderness was self-inflicted.'

'And you figure yours ain't?' Brandon asked.

Slate scratched the tip of his nose and said, 'There must've been a reason why I found that cabin, and that old Bible. Some guiding hand must've led me there and showed me the true light.'

Brandon thought that Slate was now beginning to sound like one of those preachers from his childhood. He watched Slate, deciding to let him have his say, and nodded.

'Go on.'

Slate's blue eyes raised to Brandon as he said, 'I can see that you don't entirely agree with me, Jim. But I'm able to deal with that. You see, my God is in here.' He tapped the side of his head. 'And yours is in a deck of cards.'

Brandon sat unmoving. 'You got something against gambling or gamblers?'

'You said that,' he replied, letting his gaze move to his hands. 'No, I ain't got nothing against gambling or gamblers. It's the losers and the cheats I got something against.' Then he dug his heels into the claybank's side and spurred him to motion.

By mid-afternoon, Davey Shaw had made his decision. He would take the chance of trying to get Maria away from Le Duc, today. He still hadn't worked out the finer points of the plan, but he had realized that the longer he delayed making his move, the less of a chance he had of making it work.

Bobby Hayes was still on look-out. Le

Duc was in his tent. Burn and Newbury were sleeping. Shaw had been entrusted with Maria's safety, which suited him fine. He looked at her now, her hair falling over her face.

'Maria,' Shaw hissed. She looked up at him. 'C'mere. Quietly, though.' She sidled up next to him, and he felt the warmth radiating from the nearness of her. 'We're going to make a run for it.'

'When?'

'Now.'

Maria was clearly surprised. 'Are you ready?'

'As ready as I'll ever be,' Shaw said.

She mopped her brow. 'Tell me what to do, then.'

Shaw stood up and worked his holster around to his thigh, tightening the leather thong. Raising his voice a little theatrically, he said, 'If you need to wash-up, I'll escort you down to the watering hole.' His eyes told her what he really meant.

'Ah, *si, señor, gracias.*'

'I want you in front of me,' Shaw said. 'Just in case you try any funny stuff.'

'But I don't know which way to go.'

'Don't worry, I'll tell you.' He hitched up his pants. 'Go ahead now.'

They started walking away from the camp, but only got a few yards into the pines when a voice stopped them.

'Where d'you think you two're going?'

Shaw stopped and turned around slowly, trying to act calm but not knowing if he succeeded or not. 'Ah, Lucky. Just taking the lady down to the water, so's she can wash herself.'

Newbury plastered a lop-sided grin on his face. 'Wanna get a little peek at some Messican flesh, eh, boy?'

Shaw bit back his temper and returned the other man's idiot grin. 'Er ... sure.'

Newbury walked up to the youngster. Clamping a hand on his shoulder, he said, 'Hey, I know we had our disagreement back there, but it sorted itself out, didn't it, eh?'

Davey Shaw nodded.

‘Well, how about if *I* took the *señorita* here down to the hole, iffen you get my drift? Mayhaps I can even give her a scrub, too, iffen you know what I mean?’

Shaw knew what he meant all right. ‘Sure, why not?’

Newbury laughed. ‘I knew you’d see it my way.’

Shaw looked at the woman. Don’t say a word, he thought. Then he turned and smiled at Newbury. ‘Sounds good to me. Lead on.’

Shaw kept his eyes on Newbury’s back as they picked their way through the trees into a patch of lush green grass. The sound of trickling water reached their ears through the quietness of the afternoon. He could just picture Newbury’s face, eyes squinting against the glare of the sun, that stupid grin back on his face, almost drooling at the thought of what he had in store for Maria. He knew the man and his type; he’d been around that sort for too long, and knew Maria had been right. These men were nothing but a bunch of animals, and the decision to escape was his only chance to free himself from their noisome stench. But he didn't want to kill Newbury. There'd been too much of that over the last few days. Perhaps, in his weakened state, a gun-barrel over his head would suffice. He hoped so. A gunshot now and their chances would be blown away on the wind.

They reached the water's edge.

'Now we'll see what you're made of,' Newbury said.

Maria turned to face Newbury and Shaw. The youngster stood a few paces back from the *bandido.* It was funny how she had stopped thinking of Shaw as one of them. Now she saw him only as a young man desperate to help both her and himself out of this mess.

'C'mon, woman. Get them clothes off.'

Maria swallowed loudly. Putting her trust in Shaw, she began to unbutton her blouse. Newbury's eyes were fixed on her hands as they slowly, almost teasingly, undid the buttons one by one. Shaw had to force himself not to become transfixed by the sight as well, and averted his eyes. The buttons were unfastened and Maria tugged the blouse from the top of her stained skirt, letting it hang loose around her waist but still covering her breasts.

'Let me see them titties,' Newbury growled. In anticipation of his next move, he unbuckled his gunbelt, letting it drop to the ground.

Nervously Maria held the edges of her blouse in her shaking hands. Holding her breath, she prayed that Shaw would make his move soon, so that this *norteamericano* wouldn't even come close to defiling her. But he didn't act quick enough to stop Newbury slapping at her hands and grabbing for the blouse, ripping at it, and finally pulling it away down her arms.

The sight of Maria's swaying breasts and erect nipples halted Newbury in his tracks. The excitement he felt was obvious. His eyes were wide with lust, his mouth slack and eager.

He let out a long, low whistle. 'Well, lookee here, boy,' he said, turning to Shaw. 'Come and have a look-see.' He turned back to Maria.

She stood there rigid with fear. Her eyes screwed shut, her lips muttering a prayer. She heard Newbury approach, but he stopped just short of her. There was a dull *thwack,* and a low groan. Her eyes snapped open as Newbury's heavy body fell against her, knocking her to the ground and pinning her there.

The very thought of the man coming into contact with her own half-naked body made her feel nauseous. Feeling his dying erection pressing into her stomach, Maria gagged a little on the vomit filling her mouth.

'Hold on, I'll drag him off,' Shaw said tightly. He holstered his revolver, grabbed Newbury by his collar and pants' belt and hauled him off her, rolling him to one side. Shaw looked down on the Mexican woman and his eyes drifted to her breasts. He felt his face redden with embarrassment, and quickly tore his gaze away. The sight of her firm, dusky breasts stayed with him, though, branded on his brain.

When Maria spoke, the closeness of her startled him. 'You can turn around now, *señor,*' she said.

He turned. His face was close to hers. He could smell the dampness of the grass in her hair, and he wanted to reach out, touch her face, kiss her.

She waited, watching him carefully, not knowing what it was the young man wanted from her. She said, 'We must go now, *si?*'

Shaw took a deep breath and held it for a second as he thought. Finally he released it and said, 'There's only one way out of this camp but there's a look-out posted.' He adjusted the fit of his holster. 'Can you climb?'

'*Si,* but…'

'It's our only way out. We can't risk taking the horses and leaving the defile that way. It's going to be tough, but it's our only way.'

'Tell me.'

Davey Shaw didn't move. He said, 'We got to swim a ways up river to where the watershed begins, and climb the rest of the way out and over this camp.'

Maria could almost see him calculating their chances of survival without horses.

'Can we escape without horses?' she asked softly, prompting him to make an answer.

'Maybe. Either way, we've got to give it a try.' Shaw looked behind him. The camp was still. Not a sound could be heard. He turned to Maria and gave her a weak smile of encouragement, then said, 'You ready?'

'Let us see what happens.' In low Spanish the woman added, 'Oh Jesus, son of God. Please help us through this ordeal and to protect us from this evil and guide us to our safety.'

Shaw looked at her and rubbed at the swelling above his eye. He caught a couple of the words and guessed what Maria was asking. Almost before he realized it he muttered, 'Amen.'

Jim Brandon swung out of the saddle and stretched. It had been a long, hard morning of straight riding. No breaks, no more talk after the reverend had said his piece about his past, and no cigar. He scratched his chin and watched as Slate strode around, inspecting the ground for sign. The land had become rocky over the last mile or so, and the tracks left by the kidnappers were becoming scarce.

They had followed a dry streambed west. The tracks left by the stage had been clear in the dust. Dried horse-droppings had been easily spotted too, no more than four hours old, according to Slate. They'd continued for a couple of miles before striking off to the north, towards a rocky outcrop. Then they continued on for another hour, finally arriving at this spot, where shale had covered their passing.

Reverend Slate looked up at Brandon and said, 'I can only guess that they've headed into the rocks. I don't know if they figured on being followed or if they've a camp up there somewheres, but I reckon that's where they've headed.'

'The woman's still with them?' Brandon asked.

'I can't tell, but I reckon so.'

'Pray to God that she is.'

'As I do,' Slate said without a smile. 'Every day.'

Brandon looked up to the rocks. 'Do we go on?'

'We've no other choice,' Slate replied simply. 'We've come this far; I don't suppose the kidnappers have harmed her – especially for the sort of money they're asking for her safe return.'

'But you can't bank on that.'

Slate wagged his head. 'That's right. We can't.'

Brandon tugged at the end of his moustache as he said, 'Perhaps they're leading us into a trap.'

Patiently, Slate said, 'I'd doubt it. That outlaw who shot you figures you to be dead by now, and he's got no idea about me, or the fact that we've been tracking 'em.' He shook his head. 'Still, he seems a sly one, all right. He's covered his tracks the best he can in this terrain, and now he's leading off into rocks covered in shale – very smart.'

Brandon nodded and hauled himself back up into the saddle. 'But he's got a big mud wagon to be rid of. It's going to be quite a landmark to leave behind.'

Slate smiled. 'I was thinking about that. He's got to either hide it or destroy it. It makes sense that he'll take a track that's big enough for the wagon to use, but when he's near his hideout he'll have to do something with it.'

Brandon regarded the reverend from his mounted position. Not once during their conversation did Slate let his eyes rest on one place, darting across the land, back over their own tracks and finally peering up into the mountain range. Slate had managed to work things out in a very short time, and this impressed Brandon. Obviously the man really had been a good horse soldier in his day, and the skills he'd acquired back then had not been forgotten.

Although he hadn't said it in so many words, the implication was clear that Slate expected gunplay in the not-too-distant future. Brandon just hoped he could live up to the reverend's expectations when that time came. He could feel the tension growing inside him, ready to blow like a keg of powder.

Slate mounted up and finally looked at Brandon. 'You OK?' he asked.

'Uh … sure.'

Slate favoured him with a worried frown. 'You don't sound too sure. That bump on your head … it ain't troubling you unduly in all this heat, is it?'

'I'm ready for whatever gets thrown at us,' Brandon replied gravely.

Slate wiped his mouth with the back of his hand and muttered, 'I damn' well hope so, Jim-boy.'

Slate stood in the stirrups and looked down the narrow trail. For some reason Brandon's big grey was finding the going hard, tending to come to a halt, paw the ground and then carry on a yard or so before repeating the move. Brandon used his spurless boot-heels to urge the beast on, but to no avail. Slate waited patiently until Brandon caught up.

Slate said, 'I think your cayuse is going lame.'

Brandon shook his head. 'Once we get off this trail I'll take a look. More'n likely he's got a stone in his shoe.'

'I hope you're right, because that's all we need right now. One lame horse and a hundred miles to nowhere.'

They travelled some more before Brandon called out that it was no good, he'd have to stop and check the grey over. He dismounted, held the bridle in one hand and lifted the grey's right leg to inspect the hoof.

'Yeah, just as I'd thought – there's a piece of stone lodged in there.' He turned to Slate, 'Pass me a knife, would you?'

As the preacher reached into his saddlebags, the shot that was intended to kill him sailed harmlessly by and crashed into the mountain wall.

Slate took a second or two to gather his senses, then slipped his feet out of the stirrups and rolled from the saddle, hauling his Winchester and working the lever all in one motion.

A second high report hit the rocks. From behind the relative protection of the claybank, Slate pinpointed the shooter's position. He threw a glance at Brandon, who was also using his horse as cover, pleased to see that the gambler had his own instincts for survival.

'Can you see him?' Brandon asked.

'He's no more'n a couple hundred yards up the mountain. Can you se that stand of scrub oak?'

Brandon squinted against the glare of the sun. 'Uh-huh.'

'Just to the right of that, you can just make out a narrow trail. Above that there's a rounded rock. Our man's atop that.'

Cautiously Brandon poked his head above the grey's neck and was greeted by a shower of dislodged rocky splinters. The rifleman was getting his distance down and the next shot might not miss. Brandon found that his gunhand was shaking and his stomach felt like jelly. He called out to Slate, 'What the hell we gonna do? Won't be long before he does for our mounts, then picks us off.'

Slate shared the same worry. He snuck a look under the claybank's neck and saw the reflection of sunlight on metal. The rifleman had chosen his position well – there was only one way to approach that trail and he had it fully covered. The reverend smiled to himself and called out, 'Hey, Jim. You feel lucky today?'

'*What?*'

'I got me an idea that might work.'

'*Might?*'

'*Could* work, then. If you care to take the gamble.'

Brandon was unsure, but said, 'Go on.'

'When I give the word, run like the wind back down the track yelling something like, "I'll warn the others…".'

Brandon was puzzled. 'And?'

'When our man tries to get a better shot at you, he'll have to stand up to do it. That's when I'll get him.'

'And if you don't?'

'You'll be past caring, brother.'

'Thanks.'

'Now get yourself prepared.'

Brandon looked back down the trail and sighed. There was nowhere for him to take cover should anything go wrong. If the rifleman had his eye in now, one shot was all it would take to splatter his blood across the rocks. He hoped that the reverend was as good a shot as he thought he was.

'You ready?' Slate asked.

By way of reply, Brandon said, 'Lady Luck, don't desert me now.' Then, louder, 'Yeah.'

'Right. Steady, now… GO!'

Brandon ran full pelt down the winding ledge, shouting at the top of his voice at the imaginary reinforcements to hold back, not to come any further, they had been pinned down.

One rifle shot blasted across the high ground.

The rifleman jerked upright. The bullet threw him backwards, blood spraying from the back of his head like a crimson halo. Slate watched as the sniper teetered at the rock's edge, then collapsed over the side. His body cartwheeled all the way down until it crashed in amongst the jagged rocks.

Brandon turned to look back up the trail. Slate was standing upright, smoke curling from the Winchester's barrel, and he was smiling.

Brandon reached Slate and said, 'That was one hell of a shot.'

''*nada,*' replied Slate, working the Winchester's lever to put a fresh shell into the breech. His eyes scanned the rock where the rifleman had first fired down on them. There was no movement. 'Must've been on his own,' he said.

Brandon walked back to his horse and looked curiously at Slate. He shook his head as he used the knife to prise the irksome stone from the grey's hoof. Then he thought that if the horse hadn't played up, they might have rode straight into the rifleman's sights, and the thought worried him something considerable.

Standing up, Brandon felt the need of a smoke and pulled a cigar from inside his jacket. Using a thumbnail on a lucifer, he lit up and drew deeply on the strong tobacco.

Slate eyed him and said, 'You got one of those spare?'

'Sure, come and help yourself.' He lighted the cigar for the reverend and watched the tip glow brightly before saying, 'What we gonna do next? All that gunfire's sure as hell alerted someone.'

Slate waved the cigar. 'True. But before we do anything else, let's go over and see just who that *hombre* was.'

'You sure he's dead?'

'I don't think there's many who'd survive a head shot, do you?' Slate replied.

'I did,' Brandon said quietly as he eased the holster on his thigh, and slipped the leather thong back over the Colt's hammer. He looked up at the empty rock and said, 'All right, let's do it.'

EIGHT

The buckboard kicked up a cloud of dust as it made its way through Tombstone. Karla sat alongside the Whiteheads, her face lined with worry. Her mind toyed with the words she thought she would use with the law.

She felt Abe Whitehead gently touch her arm. She looked at the old man, and gave the briefest of smiles. Abe was small, wide girthed, weather-tanned and content with his lot in life. He said, 'The law office is just across the street, missy. You sure you don't want me or Mrs Whitehead to come with you?'

'I … er … I will be all right. Thank you for your offer, and for the help you have both given.'

Whitehead shrugged. ''S'okay, ma'am,' he mumbled.

'Now, you sure, Karla?' Georgina Whitehead asked. She was tall, slim, dark-haired and of fair complexion. In fact, an opposite to her husband.

'Si, muchas gracias.' She looked over to the sheriff's office. Nervousness played across her pretty face. She climbed down off the wagon and squinted up at Abe. 'I am sure that *Señor* Sanchez will want to thank you both for your help.'

Abe waved a hand at her. 'We'd do the same for any folk in trouble, Miz Karla,' he replied. 'Don't give it another thought. You just git and help those poor souls out of their plight.'

She nodded, smiled and turned away. The Whiteheads waited until she had entered the sheriff's office before moving along.

The office gave a welcome coolness as Karla stepped through the doorway. She felt self-conscious about her appearance. Gone were her fine travelling clothes, they had been replaced by one of Georgina Whitehead's homespun cotton dresses. Her hair was a tangled mess and she felt dirty.

Her eyes adjusted to the dimness and she looked about her. There was no one in sight, but she could hear the noise being made by someone working beyond the wooden cell door. She cleared her throat and called out, 'Is anyone here?'

The sound of jingling spurs answered her and a small man with a beard stood in the cell doorway. He looked her up and down – blatant in his appraisal of her. Dutch Larkin said, 'Is there anything I can do for you, ma'am?'

Karla locked her fingers together and said, 'I would like to report a crime.'

'A crime, eh?' Larkin replied. 'What sort of crime?'

'A kidnapping,' she said in a low, soft voice.

Larkin looked at her and his heart missed a beat. Slowly he put down the bucket he was carrying and walked over to the oak desk. 'Kidnapping, you say?' He fingered his beard as he occupied John Behan's chair. His mind was racing. 'D'you know who done it?'

'No, *señor.* These *bandidos* were unknown to me.'

'I see. How 'bout the kidnapped person?'

'*Si,* she is my ward, *Señora* Sanchez.' Karla was fighting hard to keep her tears at bay.

Larkin's stomach lurched. He picked up his mug of cooling coffee and drank it down. It did nothing for the dryness he felt in his throat. 'Take a seat, ma'am,' he said. 'You'll have to give me all the details.' He picked up a pencil and a sheet of paper, and looked down at them.

Dutch Larkin knew that it was important that Karla should tell him all she knew. He let her talk away, not interrupting, just sat there playing with the pencil, making a few marks on the paper, and listened. He didn't like what he heard, not in the least. His anger would have been misplaced on her. So he sat and listened.

When Karla was all talked-out, he got out of the chair, walked around the desk and sat down on its edge, taking her hand in his.

'OK, *señorita,* listen to me.' His voice was gentle and calming. 'You've been through a big ordeal, and needless to say you're worried 'bout this here Maria. Well, you don't have to worry no more. The law'll take care of everything. You understand me?'

Karla bobbed her head.

'The sheriff'll be informed when he gets back into town, and we'll get up a posse and git after those bandits. But in the meanwhile, you'd better get booked into a hotel.'

She stood up and squared her shoulders. 'First, I must send a telegram to *Señor* Sanchez. He must be informed...'

'You can't,' Larkin blurted out.

'Why not?'

'The wire's down ... er ... that's why the sheriff's out of town,' he lied. 'Him and the railroad agent are out seeing what they can do.'

'But I must let *Señor* Sanchez know what is happening,' she insisted.

Larkin said, 'Sure, but I'll tell you what. You give me an address for him, an' I'll send a wire as soon as the lines are fixed. How 'bout that?' He smiled at Karla.

She returned the smile and said, 'That would be very kind of you, *señor.*'

''nada, señorita,' Larkin replied. He saw Karla to the door, waited there until she was out of ear-shot, then swore vehemently. It seemed that every which way he turned, Larkin had been thwarted by that gambler. 'Should have shot him when I had the chance,' he said to himself. He sighed heavily and turned to go back inside the office. He caught sight of Ellis, riding upright in the saddle, making his way down the street. He waited until the deputy had tied his cayuse to the hitch-rail and had dismounted.

Dutch said, 'We got trouble, Ellis.'

'Trouble? I'll tell you trouble.' Ellis was exasperated. 'I've spent the whole morning over at the Double Eight taking statements from Wells. Seems someone rode up there in the early hours of this morning, stole his prize pig and wounded his wife. Or was it the other way 'round? Maybe so, but I'll tell you...'

'Shut up, Ellis! This is *big* trouble!' Larkin said irritably. 'Step inside, an' I'll tell you.'

They rode higher into the mountains, up through the narrow defile where the wind became chillier and cut through their inadequate clothing. Brandon relit his shortened cigar and looked back over his shoulder. Shadows were filling their backtrail as the sun began its westerly decline. He looked up at the cloud-filled sky and guessed that there were only a couple of hours of daylight left.

It was typical that Slate was riding ahead, always a few yards in front of Brandon, but the gambler was content to have the ex-cavalryman take the point. Slate had more experience in these matters, and was more aware of the dangers involved. Brandon scoured their path, trying to copy Slate's movements, seeing if he could pick a few telltale signs of the kidnappers' passing himself.

The trail curved to the right and straightened out for a couple of yards. The horses picked up on a scent they didn't like, and they began rearing their heads. Slate held up one hand. He was holding on to the Winchester, ready for more trouble if it should occur. Brandon licked at his dry lips and slipped the thong off the pistol's hammer, easing the Colt out of the holster into his sweaty palm.

Slate slipped out of the saddle and ground-hobbled the claybank, then turned and signalled to Brandon to stay where he was. Turning around again, he put his back against the rock face, and made his way silently up the path. The trail turned off to the left and the reverend disappeared from sight.

Brandon felt sweat roll down his back, plastering his once-white shirt to his skin. But however uncomfortable it might feel, this was not the time to make any unnecessary movements. If there were more gunmen concealed up in the rocks, the last thing he wanted to do now was alert them to the reverend's approach.

The wooden butt of his Colt felt slippery in his grip. Cautiously he transferred the weapon to his left hand and wiped his right palm down his pants' leg. His hand was shaking so much that he could hear the brass cartridges clicking in their chambers.

The grey flared its nostrils as the wind brought an alien scent to upset it. Only Brandon's presence stopped the animal from turning tail and galloping away. Brandon sniffed the air but caught nothing. Then the grey pricked up its ears and stared up the path. Brandon followed its lead.

In front of them, the claybank stood stiff-legged and alert. The sound that the animal had detected came again, and this time Brandon heard it, too. Small stones rolled down the trail, headed their way. The claybank snorted and reared its head, pulling at the restraining leathers. Jim Brandon felt himself becoming tense, his stomach muscles growing taut. Sweat rolled down his face, dripping off the tip of his nose. Brandon eased back the hammer and pointed the Colt out in front of him.

He almost fired out of instinct when Slate turned the corner. The reverend's face was drawn. Brandon holstered the Colt and led his horse to where the claybank stood its ground. Slate stopped near the horses and dropped to his haunches, laying the Winchester across his thighs. He dropped his head, chin resting on his chest, drawing in deep breaths.

Brandon watched him. 'You OK, Slate?' he asked.

There was no immediate reply.

'Joe? You all right?'

'Uh … yeah.'

'Sure?'

'It'll pass.' Slate assured him. When he raised his head, his eyes met Brandon's. There was a sadness in them that Brandon had not seen since he'd looked at his father after they'd buried his mother. It shook Brandon down to his very soul.

'Did you know him?' Brandon asked.

'I think so,' Slate said. 'But I can't be exact.

He looks damn' familiar, but I can't peg a handle on him.'

Brandon waited. 'Was he alive when you reached him?'

'No.'

'So we still don't know if he was a member of the gang?'

Slate shook his head and jerked a thumb over his shoulder. 'Their camp is set up in a clearing just a couple of hundred yards yonder. I took a quick look, but I couldn't spot a soul around. Like as not, they heard all the shooting and decided to move on. But the way I see it, this track is the only way in or out of their camp.'

Brandon looked up the trail. 'What's further up there?'

'Nothing,' Slate replied.

Brandon tugged at his moustache tips. 'Then they must be still around?'

'Uh-huh.'

Brandon licked his lips. He knew what was going to come next and he didn't want to think about it. He tried to be calm as he dropped into his saddle. Slate looked up at him.

Brandon said, ‘C’mon Joe. God helps them that help themselves, don’t He?’

‘That He does.’

‘Well, let’s get this over and done with, then.’

Coming out of the shade of the scrub oaks, the pasture looked tranquil. Both Brandon and Slate raked their eyes across the camp. The cooling wind rustled the canvas tents and played with the fire’s dying embers, bringing dead wood back to life for split seconds, before killing it off again.

They brought their mounts to a gentle halt and dismounted. Slate left Ralph Burn’s body on the back of his claybank as he concentrated on searching the camp. Only when they had finished a sweep of the hide-out, and checked inside both tents, did Slate lower his Winchester and Brandon holster his Colt.

They had been lucky so far, getting to this point without being killed or seriously injured. Brandon didn't know how intelligent Le Duc was, but he seemed to have anticipated that his camp might one day be discovered, and sorted out an escape route. Brandon knew that luck was a good thing when it was on your side, but when the wind changed direction, it could be one hell of a bitch. Now that he was entrusting his life to chance, it was a different game altogether. A deadly game.

Slate had untied Burn and laid him out on the ground. Brandon took a look at the dead man for the first time. There wasn't much left of his face. The bullet had ripped off half his skull and his once-white hair was matted with dried, blackened blood.

Brandon said to Slate, 'D'you still think you know him?'

'Yeah.'

'Even with only half a face?'

'I just wish I could remember where from,' he answered. 'It'll come back to me eventually, I'm sure.' He moved across to his horse, dug into his saddlebags and brought out a parcel of muslin. 'You hungry?' he asked.

Brandon realized that they hadn't eaten since the early morning and the thought of food made his stomach rumble. 'Sure, what've you got?'

Slate managed a wry smile. 'Some home-cured ham.'

'That's fine,' said Brandon. 'I'll rustle up some coffee. This bunch seems to have moved off in a hurry – the coffee's still hot.'

The men filled their stomachs as the shadows deepened in the camp. The August nights were closing in and brought a chill with them, but they didn't risk rekindling the fire. The claybank and the grey had been watered and secured to the rope corral, content to munch on the sweet grass, but they still remained saddled.

Slate had thrown on his leather and fleece-lined coat to protect him from the cold. Brandon scoured the camp but came up with nothing more than a thick blanket to throw across his shoulders.

They didn't talk as they sat around the dead fire. Content in keeping to their own thoughts. Brandon, whose head had started pounding again, was ready to settle down for the evening. But he knew there'd be no rest for a while as he heard gunfire in the distance, coming from further up in the mountains.

Brandon and Slate looked up in that direction. 'Who in hell's that?' Brandon asked.

Slate shrugged and listened carefully. 'I counted six shots, maybe more.'

They listened as more gunfire peppered the silence. Slate turned to Brandon and said, 'Whatever's happening up there, it's a regular battle.'

Slate stood up, throwing down his empty coffee mug, and picked up the Winchester, working a bullet into the breech. He walked over to his horse and untied it, then turned around to Brandon, saying, 'I'll go and see what all the commotion's about. You stay here in case the kidnappers come back.'

'No way, Slate.'

'Listen, we've got a better chance if we split up. Right now the element of surprise is on our side. Think about it. Would anyone except to see a preacher in these mountains? 'Course not. And that will work in my favour. If it's our men up there and they still have the woman, I'll stand a better chance on my own.'

'Meaning I'd only slow you down, is that it?'

Slate shook his head slowly. 'You may be good with a deck of cards, but how would you be if you had to shoot a man in cold blood?'

Brandon knew that Slate was right, but it annoyed him that the reverend had his measure so accurate. 'So, I'll stay here,' he said grimly, 'and wait for them to turn up. If they do, what am I supposed to do, say "boo!" and hope that they drop down dead with fright?'

Slate realized the futility of further argument and shrugged. 'All right. But you'll have to use that Colt, 'stead of waving it about like you've been doing!'

Brandon said, 'I can take care of myself, don't worry.'

Slate swung up into the saddle saying, 'Pray to God you can.'

'I'll leave that up to you,' Brandon said. 'Praying's your department, right?'

Davey Shaw sat with his back against the rock, blood seeping out of his stomach wound and soaking through his cheap cotton shirt. He'd lost his hat somewhere along the way and his hair was matted to his forehead. Sweat stung his eyes, but the stomach wound hurt him more, a whole lot more.

Maria Sanchez crouched down in front of him, her body protected against further gunshots by the low boulders surrounding them.

'I'm dying,' Shaw said weakly.

'Hush, all will be well,' Maria answered, knowing that it wouldn't. She brushed away the black-bodied flies that hovered near the boy.

'I let you down,' Shaw said miserably. 'I'm

sorry for that, ma'am.'

She looked into his eyes. 'Don't be sorry. We both knew the risks. We had to take the chance... I'm glad we did.'

Shaw winced as a sharp pain racked his body. When it had passed, he said, 'I think I love you, Maria.'

She managed a sad smile. 'I know.'

He was surprised. 'You do?'

'Yes, it ... it happens.'

'It never happened to me before.'

'There's a first time for us all,' she said. 'But it was not meant to be for us, Davey. I am a married woman and I keep faith with my husband.'

Shaw held up his hand, stopping her. 'Don't make it worse, Maria. I know what you're saying.'

They let the silence creep over them. Maria worked at staunching the flow of blood from Shaw's ragged wound. She looked into the boy's face. His eyes were shut and his skin was white. She knew that *El Vistadore* would soon come upon him and she choked back her tears.

She thought of their escape. After swimming up the river for an hour or so, they had made it to a little clearing where the rocks had shelved away from the mountain face to form a natural barrier. The climb up into the rocks was treacherous, but they'd made it without incident. Shaw suggested that they rest at the spot, and Maria, who by then was exhausted, had readily agreed.

They had both fallen asleep. It was only the sound of Lucky Newbury calling down the trail to Le Duc that brought Shaw out of his slumber. But as Shaw looked through the brittlebush, he knew instantly that they were trapped. They had left it too late to put any further distance between the Raiders and themselves. Shaw continued to look beyond the brittlebush, and saw a flash of movement. He nudged the woman awake, clamping a hand over her mouth. He nodded over towards the brush and warned her to be silent.

They watched the brush closely. Finally

Newbury broke cover and appeared in the opening. Maria quickly looked at Shaw and he recognized the now-familiar scared look only to well. Looking down the top of the covering rocks, he watched Newbury carefully make his way into the clearing.

Shaw took a deep breath, held it, then fired his pistol.

Newbury never knew what hit him. He died on his feet as the .45 drilled into his heart and ripped a hole the size of a big man's fist out of his back.

The sound of the shot was loud in the clearing, echoing off the mountain wall. Shaw was surprised that Newbury went down straight away.

'He's over by that outcrop!' The voice cut through the following silence.

Shaw jumped in surprise and triggered off a wild shot. The woman looked at him. She was weary and her hair hung limp about her dirt-smeared face.

'Hey,' Shaw said encouragingly, 'don't worry.'

She gave him a weak smile. 'You say that too often,' she said.

Le Duc's voice called out to them. 'Davey! You hear me?'

Silence.

'It's no good, boy. You know we've got you cornered, ain't no way out for you now.'

Shaw knew that Le Duc was right, but kept his mouth shut.

'You hear me, Davey?' Le Duc repeated. 'Listen, I'll count to three. You throw your gun aside an' we'll work this out between us, eh?'

Shaw looked down into the brush but couldn't see where Le Duc or the others were. He shifted his gaze into the deep pines. Again nothing.

'C'mon now, boy! See sense!' Le Duc shouted. 'You do like I tell you an' we'll forget it. Give yourself up an' hand the woman over; it's not too late.'

Maria shook her head. 'Don't listen to him, David.'

David. It had been a long time since anyone had called him by his baptised name.

Her gaze lowered as she looked at him. 'He'll kill you sooner than let you go.'

Shaw was uncertain. 'Not Clancy.'

'Yes, Clancy. He has invested too much in this whole business *not* to kill you.'

'You're wrong. He's a friend.'

She snorted. 'A friend who would send men with guns after you? Is that what you call a friend?'

Now he was confused. This woman seemed to have that effect on him. He said, 'He killed his right-hand man because of me.'

'Did he?' she said guardedly. 'Or was it for himself?'

Shaw leaned across the rock, not moving. The Colt's hammer was cocked and its barrel was pointed down at the dense brush. Perhaps Maria was right and Le Duc had used him as an excuse to get rid of Franklin. The man may have been getting too ambitious for Le Duc to control, and when Franklin had continued to ride him, Le Duc had used the situation to his own ends. It made sense, but that didn't mean to say that he had to like it. The truth always hurts.

Maria's eyes were half-closed with the glare of the sun as Shaw looked up at her. He rolled on to his back and pulled her down next to him.

'What are you going to do?' she asked.

'I don't know,' he replied softly, knowing that he wanted to kiss this woman before he died.

'Yes, you do.' And she bent her head and kissed him on the lips. They embraced and Shaw was oblivious to anything other than the warmth of her skin. When they parted he felt light-headed, and knew that no matter what happened now, all of this had been worth it.

'I'm going to give myself up,' he said.

'Is that what you want?'

'What do you think? I don't want to, but we don't have any other choice, do we?'

Maria Sanchez looked at him. 'Then all of this was for nothing.'

Shaw shook his head. 'No, not for nothing.' He rolled back on to his stomach and looked over the rock. He still couldn't spot anyone in the trees or brush.

'Hey, Le Duc!'

'Yeah?'

'You got to promise me something.'

'What's that, boy?'

'If I give myself up, you got to see that no harm comes to the woman.'

Silence.

'You hear me?'

'Yeah, Davey. I hear you. Just throw down your gun and follow it out.'

Shaw looked at Maria. 'Did you hear him? He won't harm you, he promised.'

'They're planning something,' she said.

'No,' Shaw said shaking his head. 'He'll keep his word.' He smiled at her and stood up, showing himself above the rocks. He raised his gun hand and wiped the sweat off his forehead with the back of the same hand. He didn't catch the movement away to his right but Maria did, and grabbed his jacket, pulling him down.

Bobby Hayes stepped out of the shadows, both Colts drawn and cocked. He wore a lop-sided grin and his eyes were laughing as he pulled the triggers. Only one bullet hit Shaw, but the gut-shot was as good as a death-warrant.

The youngster staggered back, screaming out in pain, and fell against the mountain wall. He dropped his Colt and Maria bent down to pick it up. Holding it with two hands, she took a snap shot at Hayes as he approached. The smile disappeared from his face as the bullet slapped into the tree trunk no more than six inches from him.

Cursing aloud, he dove for cover and fired off another round from each Colt, but the lead whanged harmlessly off stone. It was enough to stop Maria firing a second shot at him though, and he scrambled for the more substantial cover of some fallen logs.

Now they had been in that position for more than two hours. The outlaws firing the occasional shot to keep their prey from moving out of pistol range. Shaw was slowly slipping away. The compression of shredded clothing had dried against Shaw's wound and Maria dared not remove it from the entry hole. The bigger exit wound had been plugged by sections of her skirt, and the cloth was now dried to a hard crust.

Shaw raised his hand slowly and dropped in on to her arm. His skin was cold and clammy, raising goosebumps on her forearm. 'Tell me, Maria,' Shaw said, his voice not much above a hoarse whisper. 'If things were different, could you have ever loved someone like me?'

Maria hesitated. The love this young man had for her was tearing her apart. 'Another time and another place, David. Yes, I could have. Easily.'

His smile was weak as he looked in her eyes. 'Is the sun setting?' he asked listlessly. 'I didn't know it was that late.'

Too late, Maria thought, *for you David.*

She said aloud, 'Save your breath. It won't be long now.'

NINE

They rode down the trail with the setting sun warm on their backs and throwing long shadows before them as the horses carefully picked their way over fallen stones. Maria Sanchez rode in the middle, her hands tied to the saddle horn and her ankles bound to the stirrups. Clancy Le Duc rode up front and Bobby Hayes brought up the rear. The two dead men, Davey Shaw and Lucky Newbury, had been left where they fell. 'Food for scavengers,' Le Duc said when Maria protested about their interment.

Le Duc sat stiffly in the saddle. His lips were pressed into a tight line and his eyes were as hard as flint. Since he had recaptured the girl he'd been silent. His mighty band of desperados had been whittled down to three, or possibly two, men. He had heard the exchange of gunfire coming from the direction of the look-out rock, but was too far up the mountain to turn back and do anything about it.

It was only by sheer luck that they'd discovered that Shaw and the woman had escaped. Ralph Burn, his guts troubling him from the atole, had had to relieve himself and found the unconscious form of Newbury near the water's edge. Burn had alerted all in the camp, volunteering to be left behind to guard their backs. He was of more use to Le Duc as a marksman, anyway. Le Duc was wondering who Burn could have been shooting at. A posse? No, there hadn't been time enough to gather one. Wells, Fargo agents? Only if someone in Tombstone had suspected something amiss, but the sheriff had seemed too preoccupied with more domestic matters to notice. He sighed heavily. Like it or not, he'd have to wait for the answer.

Le Duc looked up at the sky. He knew that it was going to rain before it got dark. They had to get back to the shelter of their tents. He topped the ridge that allowed him a view of the camp and brought his horse to a halt. He studied the place for a while, letting his gaze stop on the tents. There was no movement.

Not that he expected any, because Burn was meant to be guarding the defile. Now he raised his eyes to the round rock, peering intently through the gloom. There was no one to be seen.

He dropped his gaze back to the camp. He knew that someone was down there. He could feel it. The fire had been allowed to die out and everything was covered in shadow. But he thought he could make out the shape of a human form, stretched out on the ground, like it was sleeping.

His horse snorted and pawed restlessly at the earth, wanting to be watered. High above in the thickening clouds, a flash of lightning lit up the mountain peaks and a few seconds later a rumble of thunder echoed over the land.

‘What’s happening?’ Hayes’ voice sounded loud in the thunder’s aftermath.

Le Duc turned in the saddle to face him, ignoring the woman’s pleading look. ‘Seems we have a visitor in the camp.’

‘Where’s Ralph?’

‘I’m not sure. Maybe he’s sleeping off the gut-rot, but it’s not like him to leave his post and let the fire go out.’

Hayes said, ‘It might not be him down there.’

‘I was thinking that,’ Le Duc said slowly.

He kept his eyes on the human bundle for another minute, but there was no movement. The first drops of rain began to fall just as the dark stormheads blocked out the last of the evening light. Le Duc knew he could use the darkness to his own advantage and kicked his horse into motion, drawing out the big S&W Russian and cocking it.

Le Duc said to Hayes, ‘Keep the woman close to you. If anything happens … shoot her.’

‘What?’

'You heard. I got me an uneasy felling about this. If something goes wrong, just shoot her and high-tail it.' Le Duc would not look at the woman. He didn't want to see the shock in her face, not before he had sorted out his own rising fear.

The rain drummed against his hat and struck the trees with a gentle hissing that soon became background noise as he led his mount on. He rose at a careful pace, looking into the shadows, watching the dark trees. He stopped just the once, and listened, ever cautious of an ambush. Then, deciding all was as it should be, he rode on.

The wind increased, driving stinging needles of cold rain into his face. It blew through the trees, rustled across the leaves and bent the branches. These sounds at any other time wouldn't have bothered him, but to Le Duc, they lost their natural meaning. A creaking bough became creaking leather; the hissing of the wind through the leaves was the soft sigh of a dying man.

Once or twice he almost pulled the trigger

on some half-imagined foe, but told himself that it was only the wind.

Just the wind.

Le Duc halted fifty feet away from the campsite, hiding himself among the trees. He climbed out of the saddle and dropped to the ground, his right arm extended in front of him, the S&W Russian slick with rainwater. There was no movement in front of him and he rose to his feet. Hitching his mount to a tree branch, he looked back over his shoulder to where Hayes and the Mex woman were. He could just about make them out in the available light. He licked at his dry lips and stepped forward silently.

A bright flash of lightning lit up the area for a second. Enough time for him to see the human bundle had not moved at all and that there was no one else in the camp. He knew now that something was really wrong. The crash of thunder made him start, his nerves were jagged, and he knew that he wouldn't be able to keep this calm for very much longer – it just wasn't in his nature.

He moved another thirty feet through the rain-soaked terrain coming to rest against a damp tree trunk. The rain was penetrating his cheap wool pants and jacket and water was coming in from a hole in his mule-eared boot. The wind blew all the harder, bringing with it a smell that he couldn't identify immediately.

He sniffed the air for a second or two, then wrinkled his nose as realization set in.

It was the smell of death.

His throat was dry. He couldn't work up enough saliva to ease the dryness. He knew what he had to do. Just walk the last few feet into the camp, throw back the blanket and look down into Ralph Burn's dead face. Because that's who it surely was down there. The last lightning flash had shown Le Duc a patch of white hair sticking out the top of the blanket, and he knew then that Burn was dead. The smell on the wind only confirmed it.

Le Duc pushed himself away from the tree and took those final few steps that led him to the sodden bundle near the dead fire. He looked down, rain water ran off his hat brim, splashing on to his muddy boots. He noticed that his left hand was shaking as he reached out to take hold of the blanket before throwing it back.

Even though half the head and face were missing, he still recognized Ralph. Le Duc swallowed hard and continued to stare at his ex-Raider. He heard the soft sound behind him too late. Even as a hand closed over his mouth he knew he should have turned around and let off a shot. The gun butt cracking down on his skull put paid to any more thoughts like that.

Bobby Hayes spoke softly to his horse, stroking its head, calming it down after the first roll of thunder. He strained his eyes in the gloom, looking through the trees towards the camp but lost sight of Le Duc among the trees.

'Shit,' he hissed, and turned to Maria. 'Can you see what's happening?'

She gave him a look that said that she

didn't give a damn what was happening. Hayes swore again.

Maria shivered in the cold. The rain had soaked through her flimsy torn blouse and skirt during the first minute of the downpour. Now the cold was creeping into her bones, and she wasn't used to discomfort.

Hayes noticed her shivering and leaned across to her. 'D'you want my slicker?' he asked.

'Por favor.'

He smiled at her, teeth bright in the darkness. 'Just a minute and I'll unwrap it for you,' he said, stepping down from the saddle.

She watched him with calculating eyes. If only she hadn't been tied up, she thought, this could be a chance to get away. She watched Hayes offer her his yellow oilskin slicker, then he wagged his head and gave a little chuckle.

'To put this on,' he said, 'I'd have to untie you, wouldn't I?'

Maria shrugged.

Hayes said, 'And if I did that, you'd have

to promise that you wouldn't make any attempt to escape.'

She nodded. 'All right.'

'Now, you promise?' he insisted.

Again she nodded, not wanting her voice to betray what was really in her heart.

Hayes said, 'OK, then. But just make sure you keep your word. If you tried to get away, well ... you heard what Clancy said and he weren't joshing. I've seen him kill women afore, many a-time. He's one mean *hombre* you savvy?'

As he spoke, he worked on the piggin' string binding her to the saddlehorn. Because the string was wet, it took him longer than usual to unfasten the knot.

'You know that boy, Davey?' he said. 'Well, his pa and Clancy used to ride together. When old Bob Shaw died in an ambush on some raid or other, Clancy promised to take care of the son. Now, don't get me wrong, he *did* look after Davey – right up to the time the youngster fell for you and helped you escape. But Clancy gave the order for me to kill him more because he felt the boy had betrayed his own kin. That hurt Clance more'n anything else.'

Maria was surprised and shocked. 'I never realized.'

Hayes smiled, still pulling at the ropes. 'I don't expect it showed too much, did it?'

Maria looked into Hayes' handsome face, shining with rainwater. His eyes weren't as cold as the other men in the gang, and her heart lurched.

Hayes held the slicker up to Maria. She looked down at him, and smiled. This was her chance.

Maria stiffened her fingers into claws and raked her jagged nails down across Hayes' right cheek. The nails came away bloody, with torn skin stuck beneath them.

His mouth dropped open in shock and he let go the slicker, lifting his own hand up to the wound. The rainwater diluted the blood, but it still looked red in the night light.

Then Maria was urging the horse into a run, taking her away from Hayes, through the trees towards the camp. Low hanging branches snatched at her, scratching her face, arms and tangling her long, free-flowing hair. But she had freed herself, and that was all that mattered.

Hayes' expression turned from surprise to a snarl. Cursing himself for having trusted the woman, he swore as his hand closed over the wooden butt of his right-hand Colt. But half-way through the draw he stopped.

The end of the revolver's barrel was cold and hard as it pressed against the soft flesh of his jowl.

The voice was familiar but he couldn't put a face to it. 'Get your hand off that piece, and turn around.'

Hayes swore some more. There was no option but to follow the order. When he turned and faced Jim Brandon, his heart gave a lurch.

'I thought you was dead meat,' Hayes breathed.

'Seems like we both made mistakes, then.'

Hayes swallowed hard. 'What … what are

you planning to do with me, mister?'

Brandon gave him a cold smile. 'Do just like I tell you an' everything'll be fine,' he said.

Reverend Slate stepped away from the inert form of Clancy Le Duc and stretched his aching back. He snapped shut his small clasp knife and pushed it back into his jacket pocket. Satisfied that Le Duc was well tied, he turned just as the sound of on-coming hoof beats sounded above the downpour.

He took half a pace forward and looked into the dark trees. As the animal burst out of the darkness he brought the Winchester up to his shoulder, eye sighting quickly along the barrel. He held his forefinger away from the trigger for a split second. Long enough to realize that he would have made a grave mistake if he'd decided to shoot.

Maria clung onto the horse with all her remaining strength. He could see fear etched across her face plainly through the gloom.

Slate dropped the rifle and waited until

the animal was almost upon him before he stepped to one side and grabbed the bridle. The rain had made the leather slippery and he lost his grip with one hand but managed a tenuous grip with the other.

The horse pulled to get away but the man dug his boot heels hard into the softening ground. They had almost completed a full circle before the horse was dragged to a stop.

Slate spoke softly, 'Ease up there, lady, no need to fret. Believe it or not, I'm probably the feller you've been praying for!'

Once the horse was under control, Slate made to help her dismount, but she said, 'Wait – my feet, they are tied.'

Slate pulled out his knife and slashed through the ropes. Maria almost fell out of the saddle into his arms. He held her for a moment, enjoying the contact but not the thought of how long he had abstained from the sins of the flesh, and his skin prickled from once-remembered enjoyment.

He finally let go of her, saying, 'Let me

introduce myself. I am the Reverend Joshua Slate, and you must be *Señora* Maria Sanchez.'

'*Si,* but … but how do you know of me?' He could hear the fear creeping into her voice.

He laughed to set her at ease. 'The Lord works in mysterious ways,' he said. 'My friend should be along in just a minute.'

'Your friend?'

'The one that really got me into all this.'

As if on cue, Brandon broke through the cover of the trees leading Hayes' horse behind him, the outlaw following on foot, a rope tied in a noose around his neck, and his hands tied in front of him.

Maria smiled when she recognized the gambler, and rushed over to him. 'The gentleman from the stage, but … but I thought you had been killed.'

'So had these gents,' Brandon replied.

'Is Karla well?'

'Sure. The last we saw of her, she was being looked after by a neighbourly couple and should be in Tombstone right now, getting word to your husband about all this.'

Her smile grew wider when she knew that her ordeal was coming to an end. She threw back her wet hair and turned to face Slate. 'How can I ever thank you? Either of you?'

If there'd been more light, Brandon would have sworn he saw Slate blush.

'There's no need, ma'am,' the preacher told Maria. 'We're doing the good Lord's work is all, and that's what I do best.'

Hayes' plaintive voice cut across him. 'Never mind all this ass-kissing sentiment. You gonna untie me, or am I gonna catch my death of cold?'

Slate was upon him in three long strides, his right hand cocked and ready to smash into his face. It was only through sheer self-discipline that Slate didn't actually deliver the blow.

'As long as you're my prisoner,' Slate snarled, 'you'll keep your dirty mouth shut. Hear me? You step out of line an' I'll kick your ass so hard you'll be wearing it as a hat!'

Hayes swallowed hard as he bobbed his head. But what he said had made sense. They were all standing in the rain when there were a couple of perfectly good tents there for the using.

Brandon suggested that Maria take the smaller of the tents for herself and that the prisoners together with the reverend and himself occupy the larger tent. No one argued, they just wanted the chance to get in out of the rain. Besides, there'd be plenty of time in the morning to sort everything out.

TEN

The early morning sun filtered down through the oaks and pines, lighting the camp with a soft golden hue. In this part of the country early morning was the most peaceful, but it doesn't last long. By at least six or seven the sun was doing its best to fry anything below it. The temperature inside the large tent was rising and it was the torridity that woke Brandon from his sleep.

In the dimness of the tent's interior he could see that Slate was still asleep, as were the two hog-tied captives. He gave himself another five minutes' rest before pushing himself up on to his feet. He knew that there was a long day ahead and that they had agreed on an early start. He smiled at the prospect of seeing Karla again, and scratched at his stubble. He pulled the tent flap closed behind him and stretched in the cool morning air.

Maria had beaten him to it, and was fussing around the camp fire trying, albeit unsuccessfully, to kindle the flames.

Brandon nodded. *'Buenas dias, señora.'*

'Buenas dias, señor,' she replied. She brushed the long black hair away from her face and smiled. She had cleaned her face and made an attempt to repair her clothing. Brandon thought she looked beautiful.

'Need a hand?' He nodded towards the fire. He struck a match with his thumb-nail and waited for the flames to catch, and in seconds the fire was going. He moved back from the heat and fished a cigar out of his breast pocket. 'D'you mind?' he asked as he put it to his mouth. She shook her head and watched him light up.

She looked him directly in the eyes. 'Why did you and the *padre* go out of your way to help me?'

Brandon didn't reply directly, taking a long drag on the cigar instead. *'Quien sabe?'*

'A finder's fee, perhaps? A reward?'

'No.'

'The chance to ingratiate yourself with my husband for your own reasons?'

'No.'

She was puzzled. 'Then why?'

Brandon couldn't answer that one, not even for himself, so he asked a question of his own. 'Does it really matter that much?'

It was Maria's turn to be uncertain, but she was saved from having to answer Brandon when Slate pushed open the tent flap, yawning loudly.

'I hope you've got some coffee an' grub on the go. All this riding up and down mountains in the pouring rain's given me a hellish good appetite.'

Brandon and Maria looked at him.

'Well, what are you two gaping at? Ain't you hungry as well?'

There was a smirk on Brandon's face. 'I am. I always make it a point to get dressed properly before I present myself to a lady.'

To his horror, Slate realized that his

britches were open at the fly. He hurried back into the tent and Maria let out a suppressed giggle. That was all it took to break the frostiness between them.

The coffee was boiling and a skillet of beans and pork was on the go when Slate decided to venture outside once again. This time he was fully dressed in his broadcloth jacket, with a Bible tucked under one arm.

Maria ladled up a plateful of food and gave him a mug of coffee. He nodded his thanks and took his breakfast over to a log and sat down. Brandon joined him a couple of minutes later.

Brandon jerked his head at the big tent. 'What're we going to do about them?'

'Take 'em in.'

'You know I can't go back to Tombstone. Behan's sure to be on the look-out for me.'

Slate said, 'All I know is that we got to get the woman back to safety, and those no-gooders behind bars.'

'I agree.' Brandon reached down, picked up his coffee mug and drank a mouthful.

'All I'm saying is that I won't be able to go inside the city limits.'

Pausing a moment, Slate munched on the pork. Sweat was rolling down his face. 'Well, then. We'll get them boys to the city limits and I'll take 'em the rest of the way alone. You can camp a couple miles outside with Maria, then I'll come and fetch her. How does that sound?'

'Possible. Possible.'

'You come up with anything better, you just let me know.'

When Slate had finished his breakfast he put his plate down in the bucket next to the fire and turned to Maria.

'Now I got to let those fellers out for a spell, feed and water 'em. I'll understand if you never want to see their ugly faces again...'

'*Señor,* if you think for one moment I would be made to turn my back and hide from these *bandidos,*' she said, her lips curling into an ugly snarl, 'then, sadly, you do not know a Sanchez woman. I spit on them and their kind!'

Slate grinned at her. 'Nicely said, *señora.*' He went to the big tent and opened the flap and cautiously peered inside.

'OK you miserable sonsof. Get outside, and no monkey business.'

Le Duc and Hayes looked very much the worse for wear. They were still bound, their faces bloated with sleep and their eyes red-rimmed. Both men, still uncertain of their fate, gazed around them. Brandon stood with his back against a scrub oak and a Winchester held across his chest, finger curled inside the ring. Today, he wasn't going to be taking any chances.

Le Duc did a double-take at Brandon and his face broke into a lazy smile. 'Hey, tough man. How you doing?'

Brandon didn't answer, just stared back.

'You tougher than I thought,' Le Duc continued. 'That skull of yours must be real thick. I'd have bet a month's takings you'd be facing Saint Peter by now.'

'A bet you'd have lost,' Brandon growled.

'Oh, well…' Le Duc shrugged. He looked

over to Maria. 'Hi, sweet-thing. Still cooking, I see. How about some of that for me and lover-boy, here?'

Slate stepped up to Le Duc. 'Keep your mouth shut, scum. I'll feed you, when I see fit.'

Le Duc laughed aloud and turned to face him. Their eyes locked. And there it was again. That nagging feeling pulling at Slate. First it was the man up on the rocks, now this one in front of him. There had to be a connection somewhere along the line, but for the life of him, Slate could not make it.

Le Duc arched one eyebrow and said, 'Something bothering you, *father?*'

Slate didn't realize that he was showing more than usual interest in his captive, but his face must have betrayed him. 'What's your name?' he asked.

'Clancy Le Duc.'

'Where d'you hail from?'

'Originally? Colorado.'

Slate grunted and bobbed his head.

Le Duc said, 'You finished with all the

questions? How about some of that grub? You surely can't deny a soul some of this earth's pleasure, can you? Though I'm not sure that her cooking's any pleasure.'

'Don't worry, Le Duc,' Slate said taking him roughly by the shoulder and leading him over to the skillet. 'Your Day of Judgement is not that far off. If I were you I'd try to spend my remaining days making amends for my evil ways.'

He bent down, ladled food onto a plate and pushed it at Le Duc. 'Here, get this down you. It might be a long time before you get anything else.'

Reaching out, Le Duc took the plate from Slate.

Realization shot through the reverend like a bolt of lightning. He dropped the Bible and grabbed Le Duc by the wrist, knocking the plate to the ground. He roughly took the outlaw's jacket sleeve and pushed it up his arm.

A puckered scar in the shape of an 'S' wound its way up Le Duc's forearm.

'What the hell d'you think...' Le Duc began.

'Le Duc, is it?' Slate snarled, his heart thumping hard in his chest. 'Not *Delaney?*'

Le Duc was flustered. 'Huh? What do you ... who *are* you?'

'You mean you don't remember me, Delaney? How about Tom Mills? Or Minty? You remember them?'

Le Duc eyed him suspiciously, old memories flooding back. His voice betrayed his mounting surprise. 'Minty? Yeah. I was with the Fourth Mich – *that's* it, ain't it? That's where we known each other. You rode with 'em as well, eh?'

'That's right,' Slate said softly. 'Right up until the retreat from Lebanon.'

It was Le Duc's turn to smile. 'Well, well, well. How about that? Both of us from "The Sabre Brigade", would you believe it.' He removed his hat and wiped his forehead with his jacket sleeve. His mind was working furiously to find a way out of the ever-changing situation. He turned his back to

Hayes and Brandon, looking Slate in the eyes. 'How about letting me go?' His voice was low, not wanting the others to overhear him. 'Eh? Help out a fellow raider.'

Slate slowly shook his head. 'Nothing doing.'

'Listen. Listen to me for one minute, will you? You can have Hayes there; just say it was all his idea and let me go. Just give me a half-hour start, that's all I ask. A horse, food and some water, nothing more. Not even a gun. How about it?'

'Forget it.'

Le Duc swore softly under his breath, then said, 'Aw, come on. What's that saying in the Bible? "Turn the other cheek"? That's it, ain't it? So, how about it – you turn the other cheek, an' let me go free? For old times' sake?'

Slate stood in front of the man he'd ridden miles to capture. He rubbed his eyes and shook his head.

Le Duc pressed on. 'What's your name anyway?'

'Joshua Slate.'

'By Christ! Joe Slate!' He turned to the others and in a loud voice proclaimed, 'Hey! I rode with this man in the cavalry. He's a good man, is Joe Slate.' Turning back to Slate he dropped his voice and the smile vanished from his face. 'Come *on,* Slate.'

Slate's fist caught Le Duc dead on the jaw, knocking his head back. The preacher followed it with a fast roundhouse that connected with Le Duc's nose, breaking it and spraying blood across his boots.

Le Duc staggered and buckled at the knees. He looked up at Slate with surprise on his face. The man in black loomed over him, both hands clenched tight into fists, ready to pummel the outlaw some more, but somehow he fought the impulse. He cooled down slowly then said, 'You've done yourself no good with me, Le Duc. You're going back to Tombstone.' He turned to Hayes. 'You too, son. I'll see that you get a fair hearing…'

'You didn't tell him, did you, Clancy?'

Hayes said.

'Shut up!' Le Duc ordered.

Brandon stepped in and said, 'Tell him what?'

Hayes' eyes filled with confusion. 'About the deal?'

'Deal? What deal?' Brandon demanded.

'No! Shut your mouth, Hayes,' Le Duc shouted. 'They don't know a thing!'

Slate kicked Le Duc in the ribs. 'Keep *your* mouth shut, mister.'

Hayes' eyes flicked from Le Duc to Slate to Brandon. He felt that everything was lost and that it might go easier on him if he told what he knew.

'It was them other two fellers…'

'What fellers?' asked Slate.

'The ones in Tombstone! They'd supply us with information in return for a cut of the takings. This was the biggest job yet. See, it weren't just the money, there were…'

A fusillade of rifle shots sped through the clearing. Hayes was hit in the chest and knocked out on his back. He rolled over and pushed himself up on to his hands and knees. Brandon could see the blood pouring from the bullet wound and marveled at the outlaw's attempt to get back onto his feet. Two more rifle shots sounded and Hayes' head exploded in a mass of blood, gore and bone-splinters. He was knocked back down on to the ground. His right hand clawed at the air for a second, then stopped.

Brandon drew out his pistol and fired a shot towards the trees. Maria was next to him, screaming. Brandon grabbed her roughly by the arm and pulled her behind a big pine tree. He was breathing hard and fighting to keep his breakfast down. Her eyes were wide with fear. He tried to smile but didn't quite make it.

'Keep behind the tree, Maria. Don't be tempted to take a peek, there's a lot of lead flying out there and I don't want you to catch a stray piece.'

She nodded.

Brandon took a deep breath and chanced a look around the tree trunk. A bullet gouged splinters above his head and he ducked back.

Slate had dived behind the meagre cover of their heaped saddles, the Colt ready in his hand. His eyes searched the higher ground looking for the signs made by the bush-whackers. A bullet ripped off a saddlehorn, and the tell-tale smoke pin-pointed the shooter's position. Slate fired off a couple of rounds in that direction, but hit nothing.

'Jim! Cover me!' Slate shouted, and before the gambler could answer the preacher was up on his feet, running a zig-zag course across the camp into the trees.

Clancy Le Duc had been hit in the thigh. Bright red blood stained his cotton pants and he anchored his teeth against the pain. He was the only one left in the open and knew that he would soon be drawing the bushwhackers' fire. He staggered to his feet and made it to the rope corral. The horses shied away from him, sensitive to the smell of blood.

A bullet from a .44.30 Winchester caught

him high in the shoulder, spinning him around. Sweat and blood rolled down his face. Fear showed in his eyes. Then an easy sensation fell over him and, for the moment, he felt calm.

Two more bullets thwacked into his unprotected body, killing him.

The rifle fire stopped as quickly as it had started. An eerie silence settled over the camp. The smell of cordite and death hung in the air.

Slate strained his eyes, peering up at the high ground but to no avail. Brandon's legs were shaking as the adrenalin ceased pumping through his body. He couldn't trust himself to move away from the tree. He looked over at Slate and said, 'Have they gone?'

Slate shrugged. 'Could be, but … hold it!' He cocked his head to one side. 'Horses,' he whispered. 'They're on the move. C'mon, Jim, let's get after 'em.' Then Slate was up and running.

Brandon turned to Maria and said, 'Stay put. If anyone, and I mean anyone other than the reverend or myself, appears, shoot 'em, OK?' He handed her Le Duc's massive S&W Russian, then followed after Slate.

Brandon could hear the horses clearly now as the riders broke out from the cover of the trees and rode haphazardly along the trail. Slate was a couple of yards in front of Brandon when he spotted the first rider. The man was crouched low over the horse's neck, raking his spurs along the gelding's flanks.

Slate threw the Winchester up to his shoulder and pulled the trigger.

The bay gelding's rear legs buckled and it collapsed to the ground, trapping its rider beneath it. Both animal and man screamed in pain.

The second rider had no option but to try and jump over the downed team. Brandon held his Colt in a double-handed grip and fired off four shots. At least one hit the rider and lifted him out of the saddle with a surprised yelp. Even from where they stood Brandon and Slate could tell that the man was dead.

They moved cautiously through the cedars, approaching the trapped rider. The horse had stopped its thrashing and its breathing was becoming ragged. Slate and Brandon stepped out of the trees. Colt and Winchester were cocked and ready. The man made no move to reach for the sheathed carbine.

'Aw, shoot,' Brandon sighed.

Slate looked at him sharply. 'D'you know him?'

'Damn right I do!' Brandon hissed. 'He's one of them Tombstone deputies I told you about, Dutch Larkin!'

Slate took a step nearer to the man. '*Was*,' he sighed.

He could see that Larkin's head had been dashed against a rock. The widening pool of blood emerging from behind his head testified to his demise.

'Then the other man must've been Ellis, his partner,' Brandon said. He remembered Hayes' words: *Them other two fellers ... the ones in Tombstone...* He walked over to the dead deputy to confirm his suspicion. Feeling nauseous, he moved away from the dead man and leaned back against a tree. The sun had reached the top of the mountains and heat shimmered on the rock face. Out in the open the heat was fierce.

There was no conversation as they walked back to the camp. It was clear enough now how Le Duc had received word of Maria's movements, and known exactly where to abduct her. The only sounds came from the forest as it came back to life again. That was just fine with Jim Brandon. He now had the chance to say goodbye to Karla. Given another time and another place, though, would the outcome have been any different?

He touched at his healing head wound and was aware of a tightening feeling in his stomach, giving him something to think about. Could he dismiss his feelings for Karla so simply? If he missed out on this woman, would there be anyone else waiting for him further down the line? Or was he being too presumptuous in thinking that Karla would have him? There were too many unanswered questions reeling around in his head.

Brandon ambled over to Slate, who stood at the fringe of trees, looking at the bodies of the two dead outlaws. He looked up at Brandon.

'We'd best get 'em buried,' Slate said.

Brandon released a heavy sigh. 'Let's get it done, then.'

There were no spades to dig a grave with. Slate chose a natural dip in the forest floor and buried the bodies of the outlaws and the lawmen together. When they were finished there was no marker, just a pile of rocks to mark bad men's passing from the world. Slate chose a few words to say over their bodies, made the sign of the cross, then walked back to the camp.

The two men turned when Maria came back from the stream, where she'd been washing herself. She was cleaned up and had tried to do something with her hair.

Typical of a woman – appearances came first. He could see that she was carrying a small draw-string purse. She looked from Brandon to Slate, favouring them both with a smile. Brandon was only too aware of his dishevelled appearance and wiped a hand across his dusty forehead.

Maria stood in front of the men and said, 'I think that there is something that you should know.'

Brandon opened his mouth to speak, but Maria cut across him. 'You have both risked your lives for me, so I don't think it is right that you should he held in ignorance for any longer.'

Brandon and Slate exchanged puzzled looks.

Maria took a deep breath and went on. 'My husband, as you know, is a diamond merchant. He entrusted Karla and myself to deliver a particularly valuable gem to a client in San Francisco. It was at our insistence that we made the delivery. Perhaps we were foolish or even naïve enough to think that our journey would go unnoticed, but I eventually persuaded *Señor* Sanchez that we should go.

'Perhaps I was becoming bored, and the need to do something out of the normal routine of being a wife spurred me to make that decision. Unfortunately, the matter did not run a true course. People have been killed – needlessly so. And I feel that I am to blame.'

'No, Maria. Don't even think that…' Slate interrupted.

'But I do,' she insisted. 'Now I feel that you two are much more deserving than my husband's client. So I wish to give you this…' She pulled the purse apart and emptied its contents into her hand.

It was the biggest diamond that either Brandon or Slate had ever seen in their entire lives. The sun caught its multi-faceted surface and all the colours of the rainbow sparkled at the men. For once, words escaped them.

Brandon and Slate stood in the afternoon

heat, sweat sticking their clothes to their tired bodies, salt caking their skin, looking down at the jewel. It was Brandon who broke the spell.

'I … I don't think we'd be able to accept it, Maria.'

'For why?'

Slate said, 'We weren't in this for no reward…'

'I know,' Maria answered. 'But it is my wish that you should have it.'

Slate took the diamond from her palm and put it back into the leather purse. 'Take it back to your husband. If he has made a deal with a customer, then he must honour it. That right, Jim?'

Brandon was still in awe of the gem but managed a nod of the head.

'Then it's settled,' Slate continued. 'You take it, Maria, an' we'd better make tracks to Tombstone. There's still Apaches roaming this territory, so we'd best be on our way.'

They could see Tombstone shimmering in the distance. Brandon brought his grey to a halt and turned to face Slate.

'Well, I guess that's that,' he said wearily.

Slate only sighed, tiredness weighing heavily on him now. 'Yes. This is where our paths separate,' he said, holding his hand out to Brandon.

Brandon took it. 'What plans you got?'

Slate frowned. 'I'm making my way up to Yellowstone way.'

'What's there?'

'A National Park. A place where everything is untouched by man – a little piece of heaven on earth, as the Irish would say. Somewhere a body can ride and marvel at the Good Lord's work. Nature as He intended it to be.'

'Sounds like a good place to visit.'

'That's why I'm headed there. Why d'you ask?'

Brandon had come to a decision earlier that day. He'd considered that it would be in his best interest not to see Karla again. It would confuse him only the more if they were to meet again. He hadn't quite made up his mind if he could face life settled in one place.

This line of thought had prompted him to ask questions of the reverend. 'Just wondered if you needed some company along the way?'

Slate was taken aback, but after a moment he said, 'Why not? Perhaps I can show you the right path.'

Brandon smiled. 'An' maybe I can teach you cards.'

Slate held Brandon's hand in a strong grip. 'It's a deal.'

They both smiled. Brandon looked on as Slate escorted Maria back into Tombstone and to safety. He felt right riding with the reverend, and wasn't worried in the least about what the future would throw up at them.

Hell, with his crazy gambler's luck and the strength of Slate's convictions, why in God's name should they?

The publishers hope that this book has given you enjoyable reading. Large Print Books are especially designed to be as easy to see and hold as possible. If you wish a complete list of our books please ask at your local library or write directly to:

Dales Large Print Books
Magna House, Long Preston,
Skipton, North Yorkshire.
BD23 4ND